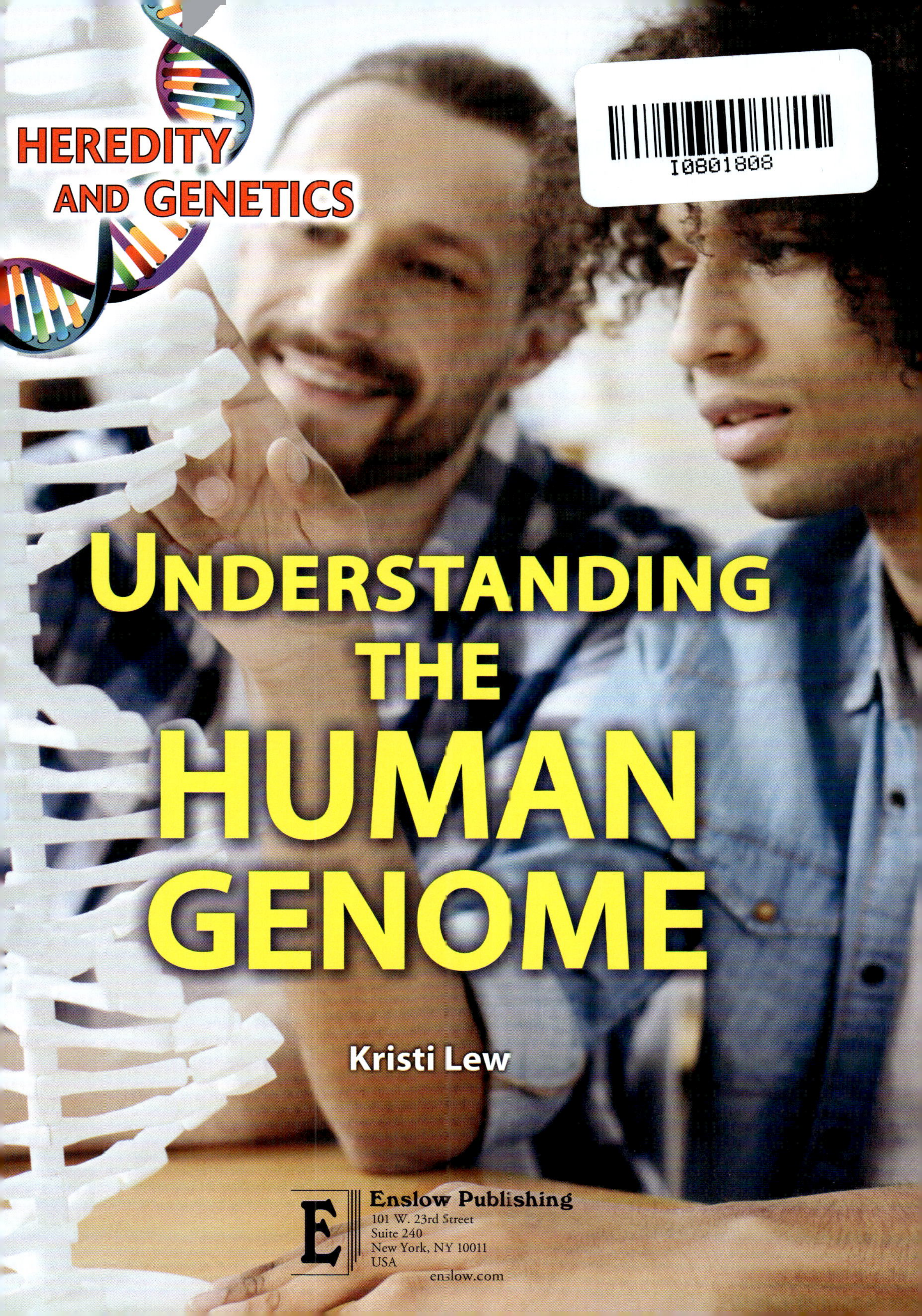

HEREDITY AND GENETICS

I0801808

UNDERSTANDING THE HUMAN GENOME

Kristi Lew

Enslow Publishing
101 W. 23rd Street
Suite 240
New York, NY 10011
USA
enslow.com

Published in 2019 by Enslow Publishing, LLC
101 W. 23rd Street, Suite 240, New York, NY 10011

Copyright © 2019 by Enslow Publishing, LLC

All rights reserved.

No part of this book may be reproduced by any means without the written permission of the publisher.

Library of Congress Cataloging-in-Publication Data

Names: Lew, Kristi, author.
Title: Understanding the human genome / Kristi Lew.
Description: New York : Enslow Publishing, 2019. | Series: Heredity and genetics | Audience: Grade 7-12. | Includes bibliographical references and index.
Identifiers: LCCN 2017058418| ISBN 9780766099326 (library bound) | ISBN 9780766099333 (paperback)
Subjects: LCSH: Human genome—Juvenile literature.
Classification: LCC QH447 .L49 2019 | DDC 611/.0181663—dc23
LC record available at https://lccn.loc.gov/2017058418

Printed in the United States of America

To Our Readers: We have done our best to make sure all websites in this book were active and appropriate when we went to press. However, the author and the publisher have no control over and assume no liability for the material available on those websites or on any websites they may link to. Any comments or suggestions can be sent by email to customerservice@enslow.com.

Portions of this book originally appeared in *The Human Genome* by Bridget Heos.

Photo credits: Cover, p. 1 Yakobchuk Viacheslav/Shutterstock.com; p. 4 Egorov Artem/Shutterstock.com; p. 8 sciencepics/Shutterstock.com; p. 10 Zvitaliy/Shutterstock.com; p. 12 Timonina/Shutterstock.com; p. 15 Science Source/Getty Images; p. 19 Sam Ogden/Science Source; p. 21 Lebendkulturen.de/Shutterstock.com; p. 24 Biophoto Associates/Science Source/Getty Images; p. 27 Jens Goepfert/Shutterstock.com; p. 28 cheapbooks/Shutterstock.com; pp. 32, 43 Encyclopaedia Britannica/Universal Images Group/Getty Images; p. 34 Marochkina Anastasiia/Shutterstock.com; p. 37 Strahil Dimitrov/Shutterstock.com; p. 40 Rattiya Thongdumhyu/Shutterstock.com; p. 44 Tom Mchugh/Science Source/Getty Images; p. 48 Simon Fraser/Science Photo Library/Getty Images; p. 50 Evan Oto/Science Source; p. 52 Dr Gopal Murti/Science Photo Library/Getty Images; p. 56 Sinitar/Shutterstock.com; p. 58 Jim Dowdalls/Science Source/Getty Images; p. 61 Sebastian Kaulitzki/Science Photo Library/Getty Images; p. 64 Y-dna data file/Wikimedia Commons/File: World_Map_of_Y-DNA_Haplogroups1.jpg/CC BY-SA 4.0; p. 65 molekuul_be/Shutterstock.com; p. 67 Steve Gschmeissner/Science Photo Library/Getty Images; interior page headers Juli Hansen/Shutterstock.com (DNA strand); interior page backgrounds and back cover paulista/Shutterstock.com (DNA double helix).

Contents

The DNA that makes up an organism's genome carries all the chemical instructions necessary to create that organism and keep it functioning.

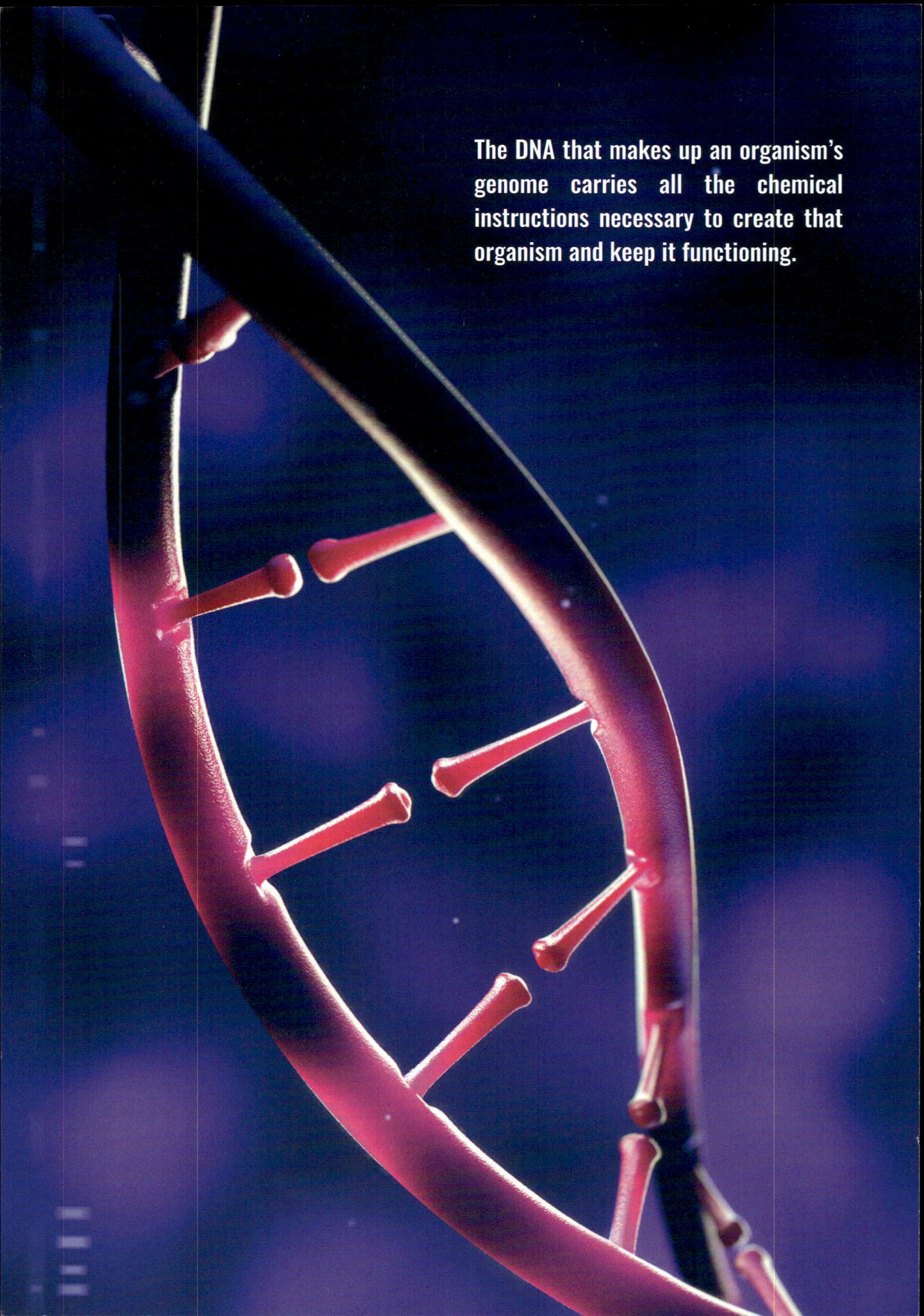

Introduction

Imagine you have all the parts you would need to put together a robot—nuts, bolts, motors, and computers. What else might be helpful? How about an instruction book that tells you how to fit the parts together to make a complete and functioning robot? A genome can be thought of as an instruction book on how to build a living thing. An organism's genome is the complete collection of its genes. Genes are the instructions for creating proteins. And proteins are the chemicals that build an organism and keep it functioning.

All organisms have their own unique genome. However, genomes between organisms are surprisingly similar. For instance, every human is 99.9 percent genetically the same as every other human. In fact, the genomes of all living things have much more in common than most people realize. Humans, for example, share 96 percent of their genome with chimpanzees. And about 60 percent of the human genome is exactly the same as a banana's genome. How can this be? A banana isn't even an animal. As it turns out, the mechanisms for making and sustaining life are the same, no matter whether the living thing is a human or a banana.

Instruction books are often broken down into chapters. The human genome is broken down into smaller parts, too. These smaller parts are called chromosomes. Chromosomes are made up of the chemical deoxyribonucleic acid, or DNA. DNA is comprised of thousands of nucleotides. A nucleotide is made up of a five-carbon sugar, a phosphate molecule, and one of four nitrogen-containing bases. These nitrogen-containing bases are adenine (A), cytosine (C), guanine (G), and thymine (T).

Even though the human "alphabet" is comprised of only four letters—A, C, G, and T—the instruction book for a human would be about three billion "letters" long. Strings of nucleotides make up genes. Most genes contain the instructions for making one or more proteins. Proteins make all the structures and carry out all the functions of the body. Each chromosome contains thousands of genes.

Only about one to two percent of the human genome is made up of genes. The other 98 or 99 percent or so is not. At one time, scientists called these non-coding parts of the genome "junk DNA." However, they have sense found that these regions have other important jobs, such as switching genes on and off. When a gene is on, the proteins it codes for will be assembled. When a gene is off, the proteins it codes for will not be made.

Mapping the human genome, a nearly decade-and-a-half-long project, was a huge scientific accomplishment. Sequencing the genome showed scientists how humans have evolved and how closely related humans are to each other—and to other plants and animals. The genome is the code of life and by deciphering that code, scientists are beginning to understand how it works and how to use the information within it.

1

The Code of Life

Where is the human genome? It resides in nearly every cell of the human body. Most of the DNA that makes up the genome is found inside the cell's nucleus, but a small amount can also be found in the mitochondria. Together, nuclear DNA and mitochondrial DNA make up the genome.

DNA Basics

The human body has between thirty and forty trillion cells total, and about two hundred different cell types. Different types of cells have different jobs. With the exception of the cells on the surface of the skin, the ones in hair and nails, and mature red blood cells, every cell in the human body has a nucleus.

Inside the nucleus of body, or somatic, cells, the genome is scattered among twenty-three chromosome pairs, for a total of forty-six chromosomes. Each chromosome pair consists of one chromosome passed down from the mother and one from the father. Germ cells, or gametes, contain only twenty-three chromosomes. Sperm and egg cells are gametes. When a sperm and egg fuse, the resulting fertilized egg is called a zygote. Most human zygotes have forty-six chromosomes.

Chromosomes are made of DNA wrapped around proteins called histones. The DNA molecule is shaped like a long twisted rope ladder. This shape is also known as a double helix. The sides of the DNA ladder are made up of sugar and phosphate molecules. For this reason, the DNA molecule is said to have a

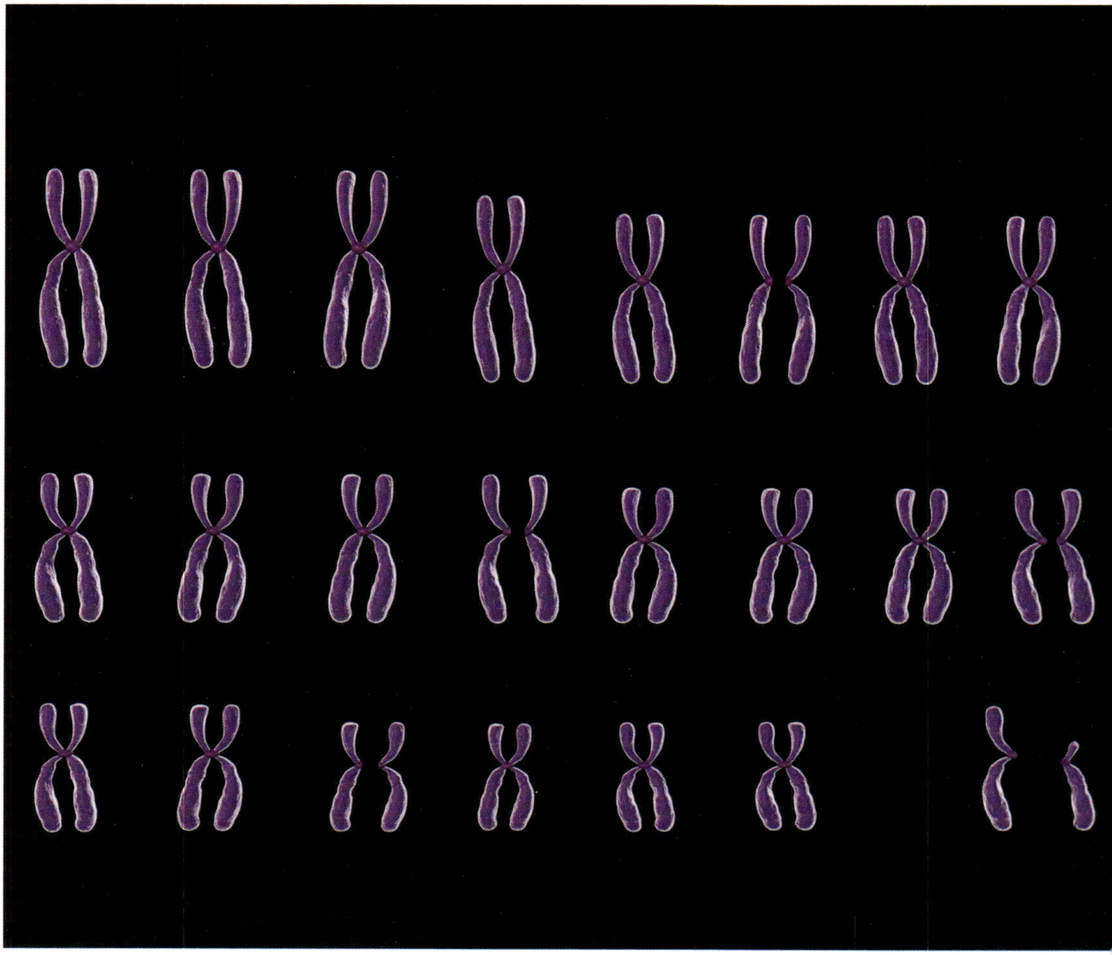

Most human body cells contain twenty-three pairs of chromosomes. Twenty-two pairs are nearly identical in males and females, but the last pair is different and determines sex.

sugar-phosphate backbone. The ladder's rungs are made up of two nucleotides—either adenine with thymine, or guanine with cytosine. In DNA, A is always paired with T and G with C.

These bases are read by the cell's molecular machinery in sets of three. These sets can be thought of as three-letter "words." These words are instructions for building amino acid chains Amino acids are the building blocks of proteins and proteins are the building blocks of the body. Proteins are responsible for both the body's structure (bones, muscles, etc.) and its functions (pumping blood, digesting food, etc.)

A gene is a sequence of three-letter words that codes for one or more proteins. Some nucleotide sequences within a gene code for amino acids and some do not. Those that code for amino acids are called exons. Those that do not are introns. These non-coding sequences make up about 98 to 99 percent of the genome. At one time, scientists called introns junk DNA. However, they now know that introns help regulate genes.

Some segments of DNA can move around in the genome. These mobile sections are called transposons. They are sometimes called jumping genes, too. If a transposon lands in the wrong place, it can have devastating effects. For instance, appearing in the middle of blood clotting genes, they can cause hemophilia, a condition in which the blood cannot clot and a person cannot stop bleeding if injured. However, if transposons land in the right place, they can switch on genes that code for a helpful new function or structure, ultimately leading to the evolution of a species.

Although a complete copy of an individual's gnome exists in every one of his or her thirty to forty trillion cells, only the genes needed for that specific cell's function are switched on; the others are switched off. For instance, in each cell of a hair follicle, the

DNA Structure

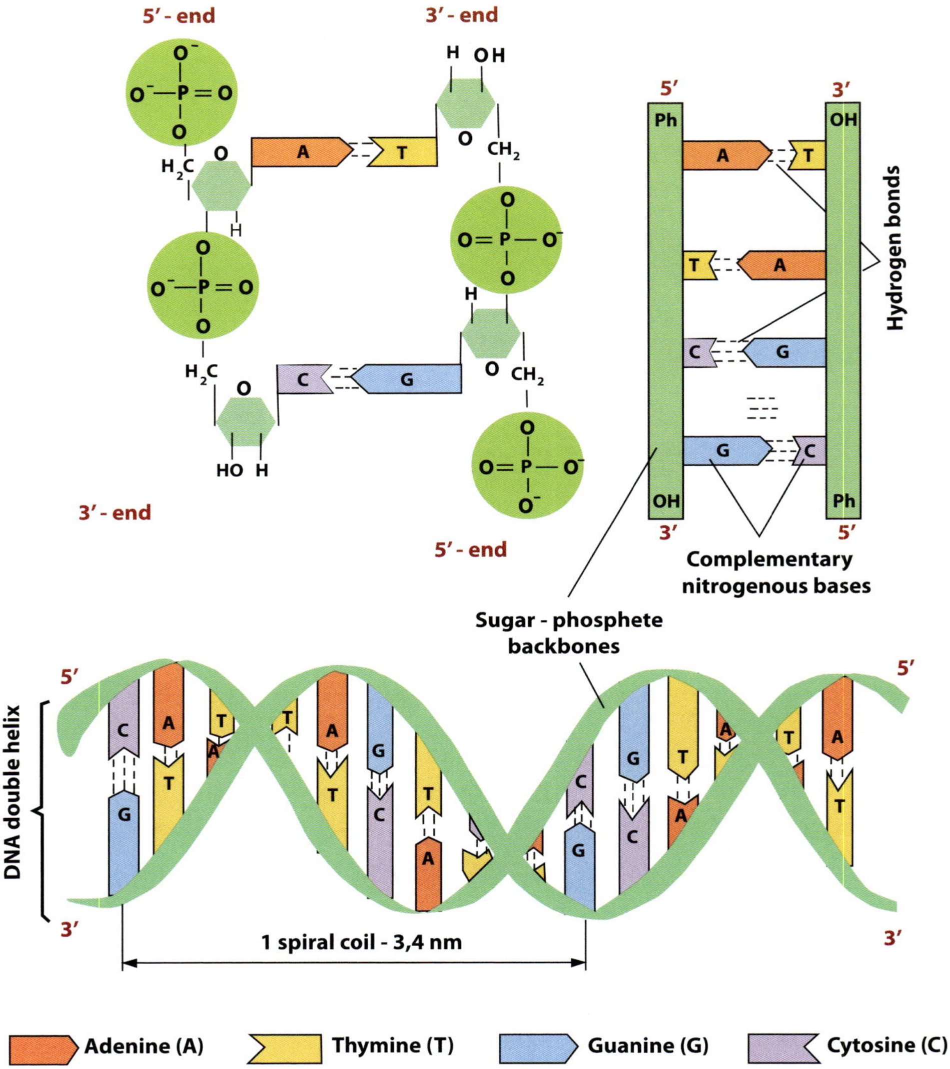

Because adenine will only pair with thymine and guanine always pairs with cytosine, one strand of DNA creates a template for the complementary strand.

genes for making keratin, a hair protein, are turned on. The genes for, say, smelling are turned off.

Gene to Protein

Basically, genes provide the instructions for making proteins. Here is how a protein is made: a molecule inside the cell "unzips" the DNA (like slicing the ladder down the middle of its rungs.) The molecule copies one strand of the unraveled DNA into a similar chemical called messenger ribonucleic acid (mRNA). This process is called transcription. The DNA strands rejoin, and

GENOMICS

Genomics is the study of an organism's genome. One way to understand a genome is to sequence it. DNA sequencing means to determine the exact order of the DNA base pairs. This knowledge is not only sought after to further scientific understanding, although it certainly does, but it is vitally important for other disciplines such as medicine, biotechnology, and forensics.

A genome map is another tool used by genomic scientists. Like a roadmap, a genome map provides a set of landmarks within the genome. These landmarks might include short DNA sequences, specific genes, or regulatory sites that turn genes on and off. Genome mapping and sequencing do not always occur together. It is possible to identify landmarks in a genome without knowing its entire sequence.

Ribosome

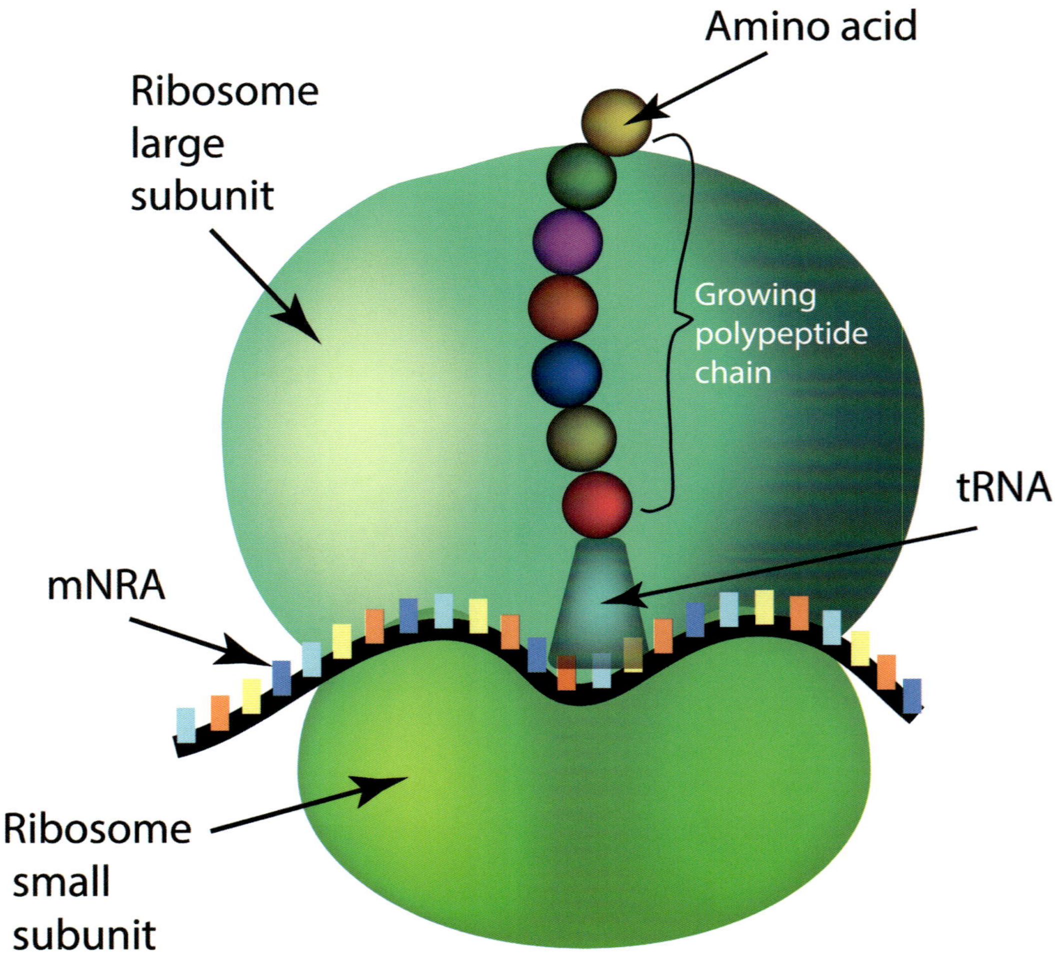

Nitrogenous bases, in sets of three, are translated into corresponding amino acids as a strand of mRNA passes through a ribosome.

the mRNA travels out of the cell's nucleus and into the cytoplasm. Next, translation occurs. A tiny structure called a ribosome translates the three-letter words from the mRNA into one of twenty possible amino acids. These amino acids form a chain. When the chain is complete, it folds in a unique way. Now, it is a protein.

There are only twenty different amino acids. But the four letters of the DNA alphabet can combine to form far more than twenty three-letter words. Some three-letter words are instructions for the same amino acid. For instance, CGC, CGA, and CGG are all instructions for the amino acid arginine. Genes make different proteins by splicing together different exons.

The entire set of proteins made by a genome is called the proteome. The study of a proteome is called proteomics. The number of proteins in the human proteome is constantly changing as different genes in various organs and tissues are turned on an off. Scientists estimate that there are approximately nineteen thousand to twenty thousand protein-coding genes in the human genome. Therefore, they expect there are at least that many unmodified proteins. Taking into account alternative splicing of different exons, however, there may be many, many more. Some estimates place the number of different proteins at several billion.

So far, scientists have identified and mapped a little more than eighteen thousand human proteins. They believe this accounts for about 80 percent of the human proteome. Most cell types and tissues have been found to contain a core set of ten thousand to twelve thousand proteins. The remaining proteins are specific to a particular cell type or tissue. Scientists think that some genes may no longer produce active proteins in modern humans. Those proteins, they believe, were permanently switched off as humans evolved.

2

Unlocking the Human Genome

While the DNA sequences of two people only differ by about 0.1 percent, there are nearly three billion base pairs in the human genome. That means that two people sitting next to each other could have three million differences. These variations are called single nucleotide polymorphisms, or SNPs (pronounced "snips"). They account for many genetic differences among people. They also tell the story of our human ancestry.

Discovering Human Genes

In the history of genetics, the study of genes, many scientists have been ahead of their time—sometimes to the point that nobody knew what they were talking about. For instance, in the 1800s, Gregor Mendel (1822–1884), a monastery leader who experimented with pea plants, discovered that an offspring's characteristics are not simply a blend of two parents' traits. A spotted black-and-white cat is not simply a product of a black cat and a white cat breeding, but rather a mixture of what Mendel called "particles," which were carried by the parents. For decades, Mendel went unrecognized in the scientific community. Eventually, those "particles" became an accepted scientific fact and are now called genes. For this reason, Gregor Mendel is known today as the "Father of Genetics."

By observing generations of pea plants, Gregor Mendel deduced the laws of inheritance and provided the foundation for the study of genetics.

Then in 1892, a Swiss doctor, Friedrich Miescher (1844–1895) theorized that DNA was an alphabet that determined heredity. Nobody believed him. Archibald Garrod (1857–1936) theorized in 1909 that genes made proteins. However, people didn't think DNA was that important.

One problem was that genetics and evolution seemed to be at odds. If genes were passed from parents to offspring, how could subsequent generations be so vastly different from their ancestors? In 1927 Hermann Joe Muller (1890–1967) found the answer. He discovered that X-rays could change genes. That meant genes could be broken down into multiple parts—what scientists now know as the nucleotide bases A, C, G, and T. These bases can be switched around, moved, deleted, and even duplicated, resulting in mutation, which is the catalyst for evolution. For example, if a gene contains a code CCA for the amino acid proline and the first C is replaced by a G, this results in GCA, which codes for an entirely different amino acid, alanine. This could greatly disturb the structure and function of the protein a gene codes for. Not all mutations are negative. Sometimes they have no effect and sometimes they make a better protein than the original. However, their effects are sometimes disastrous.

In the early 1950s, two scientists, James Watson (1928–) and Francis Crick (1916–2004), discovered the structure of DNA. They learned that DNA contained a code for building proteins. In short, they realized that DNA was the recipe for life.

By 1965 scientists understood how this code worked. However, decoding sequences was time consuming. To find a gene related to a disease, scientists would examine a clump of DNA and write down a few hundred letters every day. Then a new machine was invented that could decode a thousand letters every second. The publicly funded National Human Genome Research Institute

GAME CHANGER

The technology that changed DNA sequencing forever is called polymerase chain reaction (PCR). An American biochemist named Kary Mullis (1944–) invented the technique in 1983. Before the advent of PCR, DNA sequencing required a lot of DNA, which is not always easy to get. PCR can amplify, or make copies of, specific DNA sections. In about an hour, the procedure can make billions of copies. Once the copies are made, they can be used for many laboratory techniques, including DNA fingerprinting, diagnosing genetic diseases, and detecting bacteria and viruses. PCR was the primary tool used to sequence the human genome. Mullis was awarded the 1993 Nobel Prize in Chemistry for his invention.

announced in 1990 that it would map the entire human genome in fifteen years. The process would be called the Human Genome Project. Craig Venter (1946–), who owned the private company Celera Genomics, said in 1998 that he would map the genome in three years. The race was on.

Sequencing the Human Genome

The Human Genome Project and the Celera project were different in several ways. The Human Genome Project was funded by the government and carried out by a collaboration of scientists from universities and government departments. As a professor of internal medicine and genetics at the University of Michigan, Francis Collins (1950–) led research teams that discovered the gene mutations for several diseases, including cystic fibrosis. Collins took charge of the publicly funded National Human Genome Research Institute in 1993 and headed the Human Genome Project. Collins and his team published their findings on the internet, believing the information should be free so that scientists could develop medicines and treatments. The genome they sequenced was a composite of people randomly chosen from Buffalo, New York. They mapped the genome first and then sequenced it methodically.

The Celera project was privately funded and staffed. They didn't publish their findings, but they used those published on the internet by the Human Genome Project. This gave Celera an advantage, but was legal, as the information was public. Celera based its genome on five people: two Caucasians, one Hispanic, one African American, and one person of Chinese descent.

After serving as a Navy Corpsman in Vietnam, Craig Venter attended college and graduate school, and he then worked for the National Institute of Health. While there, he used new machinery

A geneticist prepares a sample for sequencing during the Human Genome Project.

and developed faster ways to read genes. He started the Institute for Genomic Research. The not-for-profit developed a technique that involved randomly dividing a genome, sequencing it, and then putting it back together. This technique was called the shotgun approach. In 1998 Venter founded Celera Genomics and said the company would decode the human genome by 2001 using this technique.

Collins sped up the Human Genome Project. He focused on finishing a first draft and filling in details later. He funneled resources to the largest research institutes working on the project. The two scientists feuded bitterly. Then, at the urging of President Bill Clinton, they announced together in 2001 that they had completed a first draft of the Human Genome at the same time. The race was a tie. Both Collins and Venter will be remembered for cracking the code of life.

President Clinton called the draft the greatest map ever created by human kind. It teaches us about our past, as our genes tell the story of our evolution and how we populated Earth. It has led to new disease treatments and will lead to new cures.

To most people, this is the best promise of the project. You might have a friend or family member for whom a genetic mutation has caused a debilitating or deadly disease. What if that gene could be changed? In this way, the Human Genome Project has offered hope for many people.

In addition to hope, the mapping of the genome offered some surprising insights into our DNA. Scientists had guessed a human had 150,000 genes. In fact, people only have nineteen thousand to twenty-thousand. The single-celled *Amoeba proteus* has a genome about one hundred times bigger than humans'. This shows that the size of the genome is unrelated to the complexity of the organism.

The genome of a single-celled *Amoeba protus* dwarfs that of a human. The reason for such disparity in the genome size between species is unclear.

We also learned that one disease can occur in different people because of several different mutated genes. That is why different treatments work for different people. As scientists understand genes and disease better, they will tailor treatments according to patients' genes. The genome is like a universe inside each of us: it is full of discoveries yet to be made.

3

Organization of the Human Genome

When stretched out, human DNA resembles a very long, thin thread. On average, each human cell contains about 6 feet (2 meters) of DNA. Most of this DNA is found in the cell's nucleus.

The Chromosomes

How does six feet of DNA fit into a cell that is so small it cannot be seen without a microscope? To find out, try holding a piece of string at one end while twisting the other end. As the string twists, it begins to coil. More and more coils form as the string is twisted. DNA is coiled in a similar way. This supercoiling allows the molecule to take up less space.

DNA is twisted around histones and subdivided into forty-six chromosomes. Scientists have numbered twenty-two pairs of these chromosomes from largest to smallest. However, due to an early mistake, chromosome 21 is actually smaller than chromosome 22. Chromosomes one through twenty-two are called autosomes and are virtually the same in all humans. The last pair of chromosomes are the sex chromosomes. Instead of being numbered, the sex chromosomes are designated by the letters

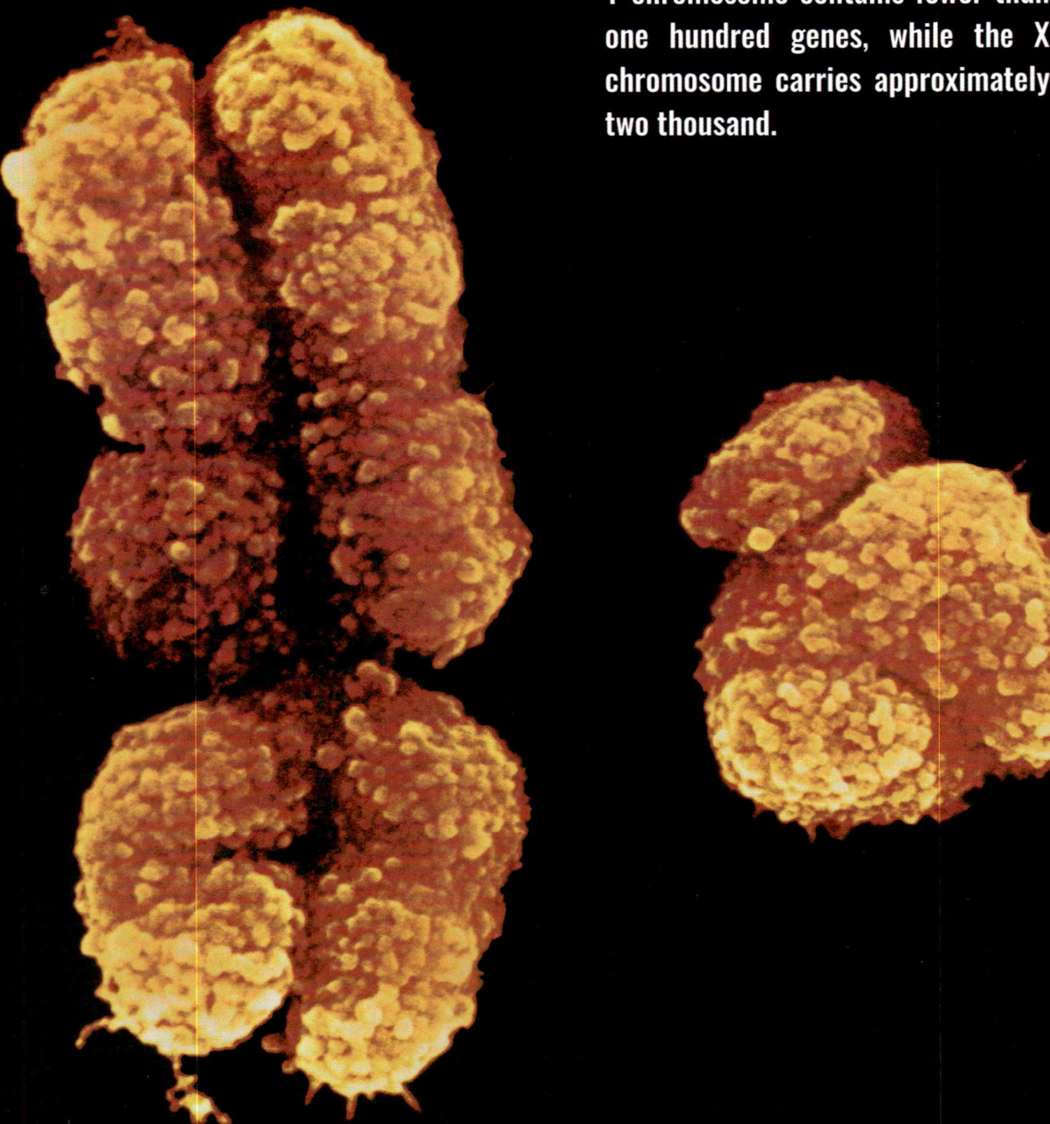

Males have one X chromosome (*left*) and one Y chromosome (*right*). The Y chromosome contains fewer than one hundred genes, while the X chromosome carries approximately two thousand.

X and Y. Y is the smallest chromosome. X lies, in size, between chromosomes 7 and 8. Women have two X chromosomes. Men have one X and one Y.

The human genome is not necessarily organized by gene function. Unrelated genes cluster on some chromosomes, and genes that contribute to one trait are on different chromosomes. Our sense of smell, for instance, has a thousand genes scattered throughout the genome. Only about 40 percent are functional, probably because we no longer rely on smell as much as our ancestors did.

Most humans have forty-six chromosomes—two chromosome number 1s, two chromosome 2s, and so on, consisting of twenty-two autosome pairs and one pair of sex chromosomes. It's no coincidence that humans have two of each chromosome. Everyone receives one copy from each parent. Having two copies of a gene can be beneficial. If one gene is faulty, the working gene can take its place. This isn't always the case. In dominant diseases, one faulty gene causes a problem. Also, since boys have just one X chromosome, a recessive gene on this chromosome can be expressed. That is why some genetic conditions, such as color blindness, are more common in men than women.

More than half of all early pregnancy losses are due to a chromosomal abnormality. However, many babies are born with less or more than forty-six chromosomes. Depending on which chromosome is tripled or reduced to one, the condition can cause mild to severe physical or mental disabilities. Turner's syndrome is a chromosomal disorder in which a baby girl is born with only one complete X chromosome. This syndrome may cause slow growth, delayed puberty, and heart abnormalities. A child born with an extra chromosome 18 has trisomy 18, or Edwards' syndrome. Edwards' syndrome is fatal and has no treatment.

ADAPTING TO LOW OXYGEN

All human cells need oxygen to function properly. Yet, some people live at altitudes where the concentration of oxygen is quite low. How do these peoples' genomes differ from those of people who live at sea level? To find out, scientists have studied two high-altitude populations—Andean and Tibetan highlanders.

Researchers have found that both populations carry genetic mutations that allow them to thrive in an environment that would make other people sick. However, they do not carry the same genetic mutation or even mutations that have the same effect on the body.

Red blood cells carry oxygen from the lungs throughout the body. Having too many red blood cells makes the blood thicker and stickier, increasing the risk of clots, strokes, and high blood pressure. Tibetans have a mutation that limits their production of red blood cells. Andeans, on the other hand, appear to have genes that protect them from the negative consequences.

A baby born with this disorder often dies within a year. Those who survive to childhood or teen years deal with severe medical problems and developmental disabilities.

The most commonly occurring chromosomal condition is Down syndrome, in which a baby is born with a third copy of chromosome 21. For this reason, Down syndrome is also known as trisomy 21. About one in every seven hundred babies is born with Down syndrome. People with Down syndrome may have mild to moderate learning disabilities, developmental delays, and distinguishing physical characteristics. With early intervention and schooling tailored to their individual needs, they often finish high school and go on to work full time or attend college.

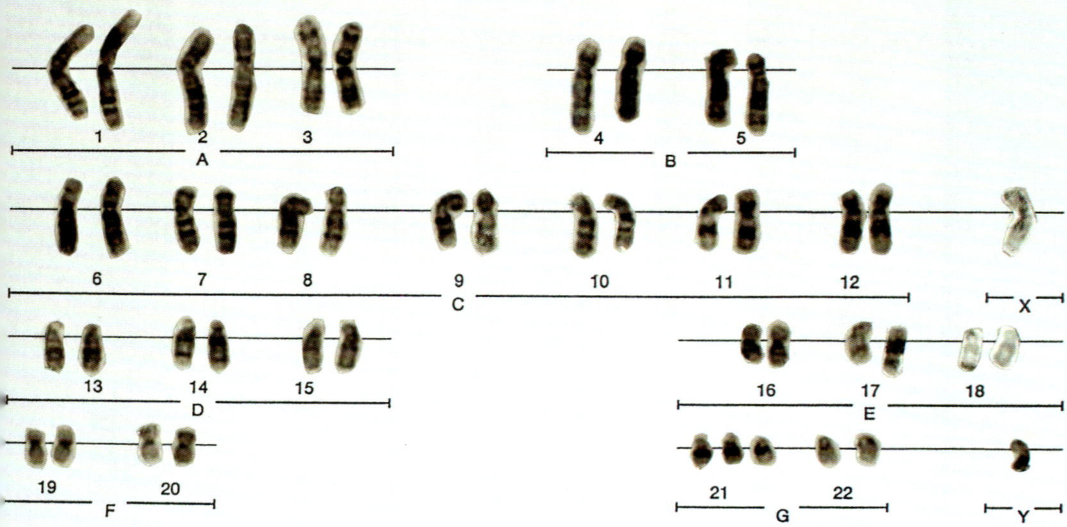

A person with Down syndrome has an extra copy of chromosome 21. This image of a person's chromosomes, called a karyotype, shows the chromosomes of a male with Down syndrome.

While a person's stress response is at least partially determined by his or her genes, lifestyle choices can help diminish the harmful effects that excessive stress can have on the body.

Nature or Nurture

In news stories, genes are often linked to diseases, personality traits, or intelligence. These genes are the celebrities of the genome. However, most genes do ordinary—but important—jobs. They are the recipes for proteins that make the body and allow it to function normally.

It's understandable that people are more interested in more widely discussed or popular genes. Understanding disease-related genes may lead to new treatments. And most people would like to know why they are good at math or bad at it, shy or friendly, cautious or impulsive. Is it in their genes? Or does their environment shape them?

In other words, which is more important, nature or nurture? Nature refers to genes. Nurture concerns upbringing, friends, nutrition, and other factors in the environment. The truth is: nurture and nature are not at odds. They are intertwined. Genes are designed to adapt to the environment—and may even create the environment.

For example, have you noticed that some people are stressed out by the smallest things and others can handle big problems amazingly well? As it turns out, some people may be more genetically susceptible to stress than others. When something out of our control happens—such as a car wreck, a breakup with a partner, or a family crisis—a gene called CYP17, one of many genes involved with stress responses, makes an enzyme that converts cholesterol to several hormones, including cortisol. Cortisol changes the configuration of the brain. It makes the ears, nose, and eyes more sensitive. It lessens the number of white blood cells, making a person more susceptible to sickness and disease. Research suggests that some laid back people either produce or react to cortisol to a lesser extent than their high-strung counterparts.

The good news is that even in high stress situations, people can do something about it—not on the inside but on the outside. While a person may not be able to change his or her genes, he or she can change an environment and how to respond to it. For instance, if students dislike school, they might not be able to transfer, but they can take classes they enjoy, seek out friends who are supportive, and be active in after school activities.

4

Human Inheritance

Humans reproduce through sexual reproduction. This type of reproduction allows for a mixture of genes to be passed from one generation to the next. In contrast, asexual reproduction involves only one parent and the offspring receives an exact copy of the parent's genome. This makes the offspring a clone of its parents. Asexual reproduction has one major disadvantage: because there is no genetic variation, environmental changes that affect one organism may affect all of them.

How Human Heredity Works

Genes are passed down from parent to child on chromosomes. A normal cell—one with forty-six chromosomes, or two sets of twenty-three—goes through a process called meiosis. During meiosis, the chromosomes swap genetic information, and the cell divides. Finally, each gamete is left with just twenty-three chromosomes. These chromosomes are a unique and random mixture of the mother's or father's genes. They may include genes that were not expressed in the mother or father but will be in the child. In fact, every man or woman can produce eight million possible gametes. Together, they can create sixty-four trillion

Meiosis, or sex cell division

During meiosis, homologous chromosomes swap sections of DNA. This process creates gametes in which the parental genes have been shuffled. This random assortment of genes creates genetic variation in the offspring.

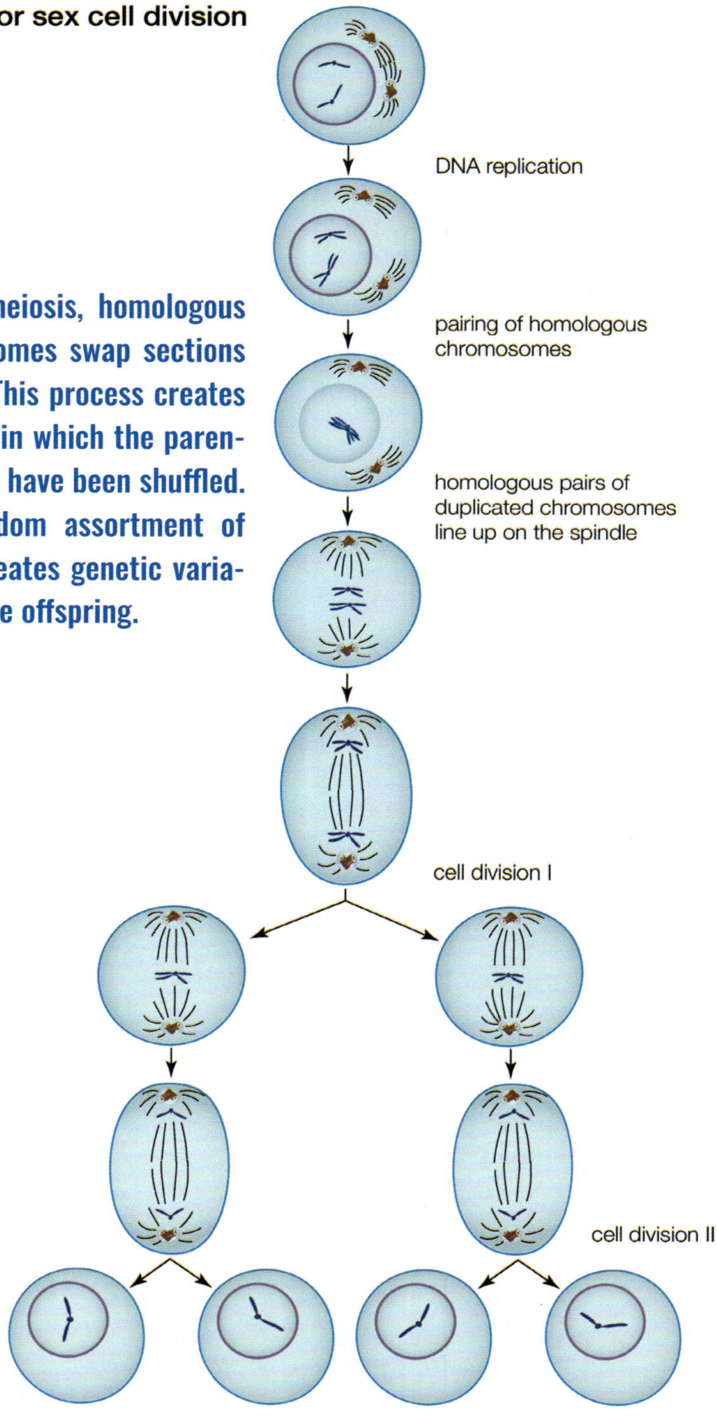

different possible children. (Which is why two siblings may be very different from each other.)

When the nucleus of the sperm (gamete one) meets the nucleus of the egg (gamete two), they fuse to form a new cell, the zygote. The zygote has forty-six chromosomes—twenty-three from each parent. These chromosomes hold all of the offspring's genes. The zygote divides several times, going through the stages of embryonic development. Finally, it is a newborn with about ten trillion cells (which will become a grownup with one hundred trillion cells or so). Each of these cells, with a couple exceptions, carries all of the chromosome pairs: the entire genome. However, some genes are never expressed. For instance, one in twenty-five

EPIGENETICS

Not all changes in phenotype are a result of changes in genotype. In other words, some heritable variations are a result of genes being turned on or off without any changes occurring in the DNA sequence. The study of heritable changes in gene expression is called epigenetics, which literally means "on top of genetics."

Some epigenetic changes occur naturally. Genes that need to be expressed during fetal development, for example, are turned off later in life. However, environmental factors, such as pollutants, can also cause genes to be turned off. When this happens to genes that usually suppress tumor formation or repair mistakes in the copying of DNA, diseases such as cancer may result.

HUMAN FERTILIZATION

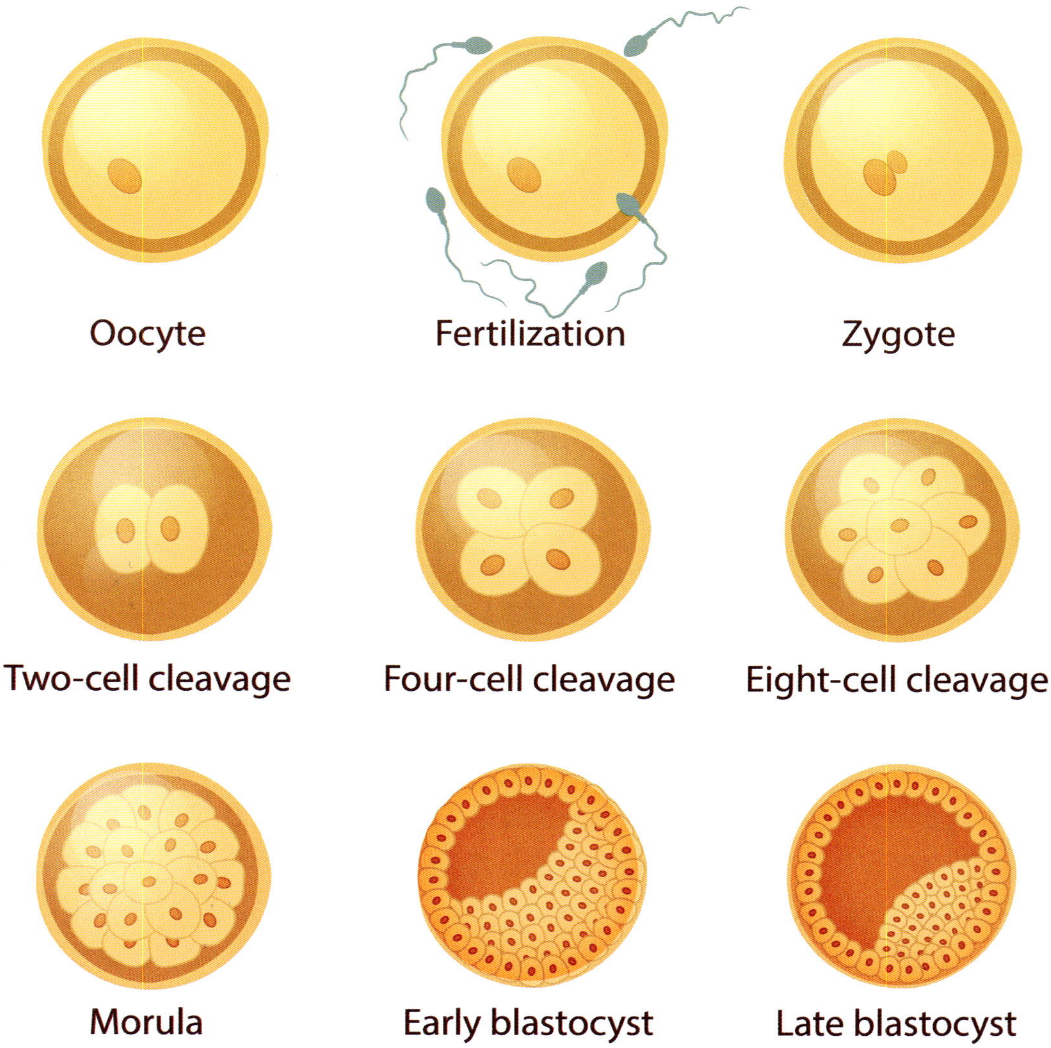

When an oocyte, or egg, is fertilized by a sperm cell, a zygote is formed. The zygote divides to form a solid ball of cells called a morula. A blastocyst forms as the embryo continues to develop.

European Americans is a genetic carrier for cystic fibrosis. Unless both parents carry the mutated gene, a baby has no chance of getting the disease. However, the child might be a carrier like his or her mom or dad.

A genotype refers to a person's entire genetic makeup. A phenotype is the part of the genome that is expressed—in other words, what you see. What determines which genes are expressed and which aren't? Many factors do.

Some genes are dominant and some are recessive. Cystic fibrosis is recessive, which means a person must inherit two mutated genes—one from mom and one from dad—to have the disease. If only one copy of the mutated gene is passed down, he or she will be a carrier. On the other hand, a disease caused by a dominant gene will develop if the mutation from just one parent is passed down. Huntington's disease, for example, is inherited in a dominant fashion.

The gene that causes Huntington's disease is found on chromosome 4. Within this gene is a repeat of the DNA base sequence CAG. Normally, this repeat occurs between ten and thirty-five times. If, however, this sequence is repeated thirty-nine times or more, Huntington's disease will develop. The more times the sequence is repeated, the earlier the disease will likely develop and with more severe symptoms. (At least one other gene also affects the age of onset.) Huntington's appears in adulthood and causes loss of balance, depression, hallucinations, delusions, and ultimately death. If a parent has Huntington's, the odds are 50/50 that a child will develop the disease, too. Scientists are trying to find a cure.

A so-called crime gene was found in a Dutch family. A pregnant woman asked her doctor if her child would be mentally disabled, like many men in her family. The doctor learned that the men were not, in fact, mentally disabled but instead violent. They had a single point mutation on the gene MAO on the X chromosome. Typically, this gene breaks down serotonin, a neurotransmitter in the brain involved in regulating mood, impulsivity, and inhibition of responses. When this gene doesn't function well, it can impair the fight or flight response and the response to stress. Mutations in the gene can cause aggression, but not always. The mutation is rare and definitely not the cause of all crime. Instead of relying on genetic causes to explain crime, researchers recommend focusing on social factors, such as childcare and education.

Combining Genes and the Environment

Other genes are additive, meaning they combine to create a certain trait. Take height, for instance. Between four hundred and seven hundred genes affect how tall a person will be. The genes inherited from a mother and those inherited from a father combine in ways scientists do not completly understand to create a person's height. In boys, a gene on the Y chromosome is thought to increase height by about three inches. A family might have one boy who is six foot two and another who is five foot seven. This is because each parent passes on genes to the child randomly. The shorter son likely inherited gene variations from relatives who were shorter. Whereas the taller son probably got genes passed down from taller relatives. While scientists believe that height is almost completely determined by genetics, environmental factors, such as nutrition and exposure to some medications, are also believed to play a part in how tall a person becomes.

Additive genes make up many traits, including several personality characteristics. If a person tends to take risks, that may be due to about eleven different genes, including D4DR on chromosome 11. In the middle of this gene, a sequence of letters

Thrill-seeking, such as going bungee jumping, tends to run in families because this type of behavior is at least partially influenced by genetics. However, environment may play a large part in whether someone is willing to take a risk, too.

repeats two to eleven times. The larger the number of repeats, the more ineffectively a person's brain captures dopamine, a neurotransmitter or chemical involved in motivation and pleasure. That means the person needs to do something adventurous to get the same dopamine buzz others get from doing ordinary things. Risk-seeking is about 60 percent heritable. That means that even if a person is genetically inclined toward risk taking, he or she may be influenced by environmental factors such as friends and upbringing, and never take risks. Or he or she might take calculated risks, such as quitting a job to start a business, but not foolish ones, such as driving recklessly.

Personality traits may be hereditary in part, but they're not set in stone. People's environment and even their self-perception play a role. Many learning disabilities are genetic. However, as these students learn study skills, they often wind up getting better grades than students who don't have a disability. Some people may be prone to stress. But by exercising, surrounding themselves with good friends, and choosing enjoyable careers, they can limit how often their cortisone-releasing genes go into overdrive. Shyness is probably genetic, but once people accept their shyness as part of their genetic makeup, they usually feel more comfortable around people.

5

Human Ancestry

The human genome reveals a lot about how humans have evolved over time. By tracing tiny changes in the DNA sequences between groups of people, scientists can even trace the migration patterns of our ancient ancestors.

The Evolution of *Homo Sapiens*

Five hundred thirty million years ago, humans descended from a type of flatworm. We were able to evolve into new species—with arms and legs—thanks, in part, to our HOX genes. HOX genes are laid out head to toe and dictate how the fetus develops in the womb, and which genes are expressed and when. They also help species to evolve into new species, also by regulating gene expression, or which genes are on and which are off.

Eventually, we became primates. We shared a common ancestor with chimpanzees six to seven million years ago. Chimpanzees have twenty-four chromosome pairs compared to our twenty-three. At some point, our second and third chromosomes fused. Amazingly, our DNA is 99 percent the same as chimpanzees. However, because we have three billion units, that leaves us with thirty million differences.

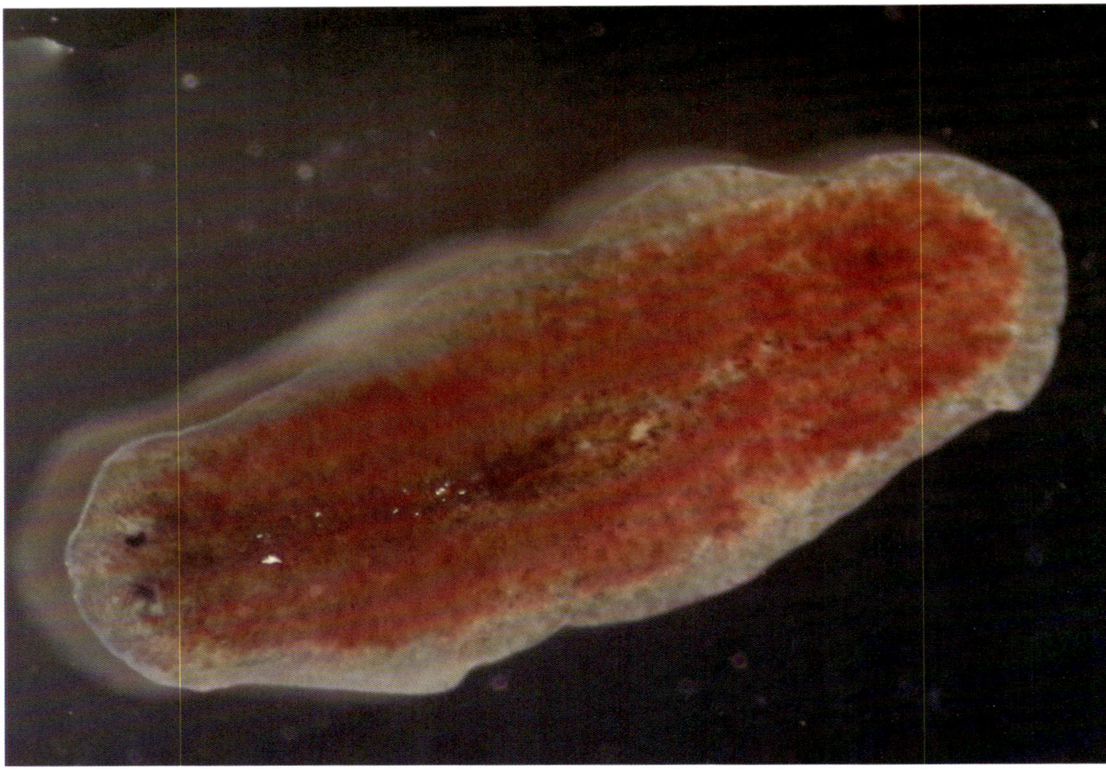

Using genes shared between organisms, scientists have been able to trace the origin of all bilateral animals (those with a left and a right side), including humans, back to a primitive type of flatworm.

The primate family tree gave birth to several species; our branch evolved into *Homo sapiens*. *Homo sapiens* are a newer species, only around two hundred thousand years old. About 195,000 years ago, all humans living today shared a common female ancestor known as Mitochondrial Eve. She wasn't the only woman living back then. However, she was the only one to pass on her mitochondrial DNA to future generations of women. Children of the other women living at the time either did not have offspring or their lines died out at some point before modern times. Mitochondria are structures within cells that produce energy. Interestingly, they contain a small loop of DNA. After fertilization, mitochondrial DNA from the male's sperm is destroyed. As a result, all humans carry only their mother's mitochondrial DNA. For this reason, mitochondrial DNA can be used to trace generations back to our common maternal ancestors.

The last shared male ancestor, Y-Chromosomal Adam, is thought to have lived around two hundred thousand years ago, too. He passed on his genetic markers through the Y chromosome to future generations of men. Genetic Adam and Eve both lived in Africa at about the same time, but they weren't necessarily a couple. Instead, scientists believe there were many couples living at that time. However, like mitochondrial Eve, Y-chromosomal Adam's genes are the only ones to survive to modern times.

About 130,000 years ago, an ice age turned Africa from lush land into a desert. The entire human population dwindled to about two thousand—the size of the population of some high schools. This caused a genetic bottleneck resulting in gene mutation spreading through the population faster, speeding up evolution, and giving birth to a human species that now has very little genetic diversity. The wildebeest in Kenya alone have twice as much genetic variation as the seven billion humans all over the world. Among humans, Africa is the most genetically diverse continent in the world since our species has been living there the longest.

By about fifty thousand years ago, some human ancestors migrated out of Africa. Our genome tells the history of this migration. About every ten thousand years, a mutation occurs on mitochondrial DNA (circular DNA inside mitochondria.) If two people share all but one mutation, their closest ancestor lived ten thousand years ago. Native Americans share a common ancestor

THE EVOLUTION OF MITOCHONDRIA

All living things can be broken down into two groups—prokaryotes and eukaryotes. Prokaryotes are relatively simple single-celled organisms with no nucleus. Their genes lie on a circular strand of DNA found within the cell's cytoplasm. Eukaryotes are more complex and their cells have a nucleus and organelles.

At one time, scientists believe that mitochondria were independent prokaryotes—most likely a type of bacterium. Then, at some point in the past, another type of single-celled organism engulfed a mitochondrion—probably as a meal. Instead of being digested, the mitochondrion to up permanent residence inside this other organism, a situation called endosymbiosis.

with a clan living in Siberia twenty thousand years ago. Other clans may have traveled to America, too, but only the descendants of one clan survived. Forty thousand years ago, Native Americans and Europeans shared a common ancestor in Central Asia.

Genetic Drift and Natural Selection

When *Homo sapiens* left Africa and spread throughout the world, they likely encountered other species of humans, including Neanderthals in Europe. For years, scientists debated whether Europeans mated with Neanderthals, in which case, modern

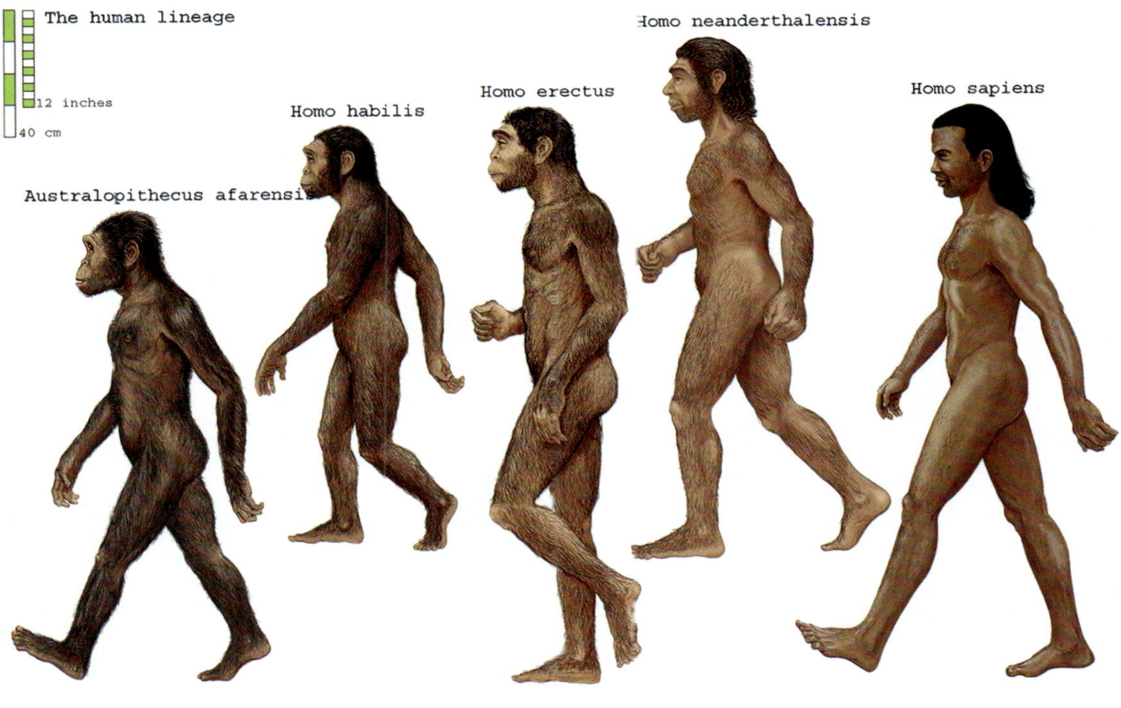

Fossil evidence reveals many species of early humans. The *Australopithecus* group walked upright but also climbed trees. The *Homo* group, which includes modern *Homo sapiens*, was the first to use tools and to venture out of Africa.

Homo neanderthalensis is an extinct human species. This ancient relative of modern humans lived in Europe and central Asia about four hundred thousand to forty thousand years ago.

Europeans would have some Neanderthal genes. With knowledge of the genome, scientists were able to test that theory. Looking at the mitochondrial DNA of Neanderthal remains found in Croatia, scientists didn't see genetic markers that would indicate widespread interbreeding between species. They have since mapped the Neanderthal genome, confirming that *Homo sapiens* and Neanderthals didn't mate on a large scale.

However, archaeological evidence of tools and burial sites show that Neanderthals were similar to our ancestors in intelligence and culture. The Neanderthal genome indicates that they, too, had the FOXP2 gene, meaning they probably talked. So why didn't the two species hit it off? Perhaps they viewed each other as separate species (which they were) and, thus, too different. Or they simply might not have encountered each other that often, as the Neanderthal numbers were dwindling at the time.

Physical differences among *Homo sapiens* developed ten thousand years after the species left Africa. Genetic drift—or chance—played a role. Imagine if five clans set out for new land. Due to a difficult journey, harsh climate, and fierce predators, maybe only one clan survived. That clan would have had certain genes that caused traits neither helpful nor harmful—such as red hair. Those traits would be prevalent in future generations.

Natural selection, of course, played a large role in the traits humans developed. It works like this: a mutation causes a gene to either stop making a protein or to make a protein with a different structure. This can be helpful, harmful, helpful and harmful, or have no effect. If the mutation boosts the number of offspring, it will spread through the population. This is natural selection. When a gene has more mutations in its coding region than in its non-coding region, natural selection probably influenced the genetic change.

As primates developed, natural selection helped them to develop an upright gait, bigger brains, and some of the instincts we still have today. Once *Homo sapiens* evolved and spread out around the planet, natural selection worked on individual groups of people. Consider milk. Most mammals can only drink milk (their mother's) as babies. Later, their bodies do not produce the enzyme, called lactase, to break down lactose, the sugar in milk. Thousands of years ago, cattle herders developed a mutation to a gene called LCT, which allowed them to digest milk into adulthood. The mutation happened randomly, but the extra calories resulted in milk drinkers having more children. (People who were not cattle herders may have also had this mutation, but because they didn't have milk available, it didn't result in more children.) Today 70 percent of the cattle herders' descendants can drink milk, as opposed to only 30 percent of people who do not descend from cattle herders.

6

Changes in the Genome

Even before the Human Genome Project sequenced the entire genome, doctors routinely used genetic testing to identify carriers of certain genetic diseases, screen newborns for treatable inherited conditions, and diagnose some types of cancer. Since the completion of the Project, however, advances in genomic medicine have increased tremendously.

Genetic Diseases

Every time a cell divides, the DNA in the nucleus replicates. During this duplication, all three billion letters of the genome are copied, and sometimes mistakes occur. Many of these mutations make no difference. Either they occur on DNA that doesn't encode for proteins, or the new gene is equally capable of making a protein. Other times, the mutations are helpful, as in the case of the milk gene. But sometimes, one wrong letter can have tragic results. When errors occur in somatic cells, which do not produce gametes, the mistakes are not passed on to future generations. When they occur in germ cells, which produce gametes for reproduction (sperm and egg), the mutated genes become hereditary. Errors in single genes are responsible for more than

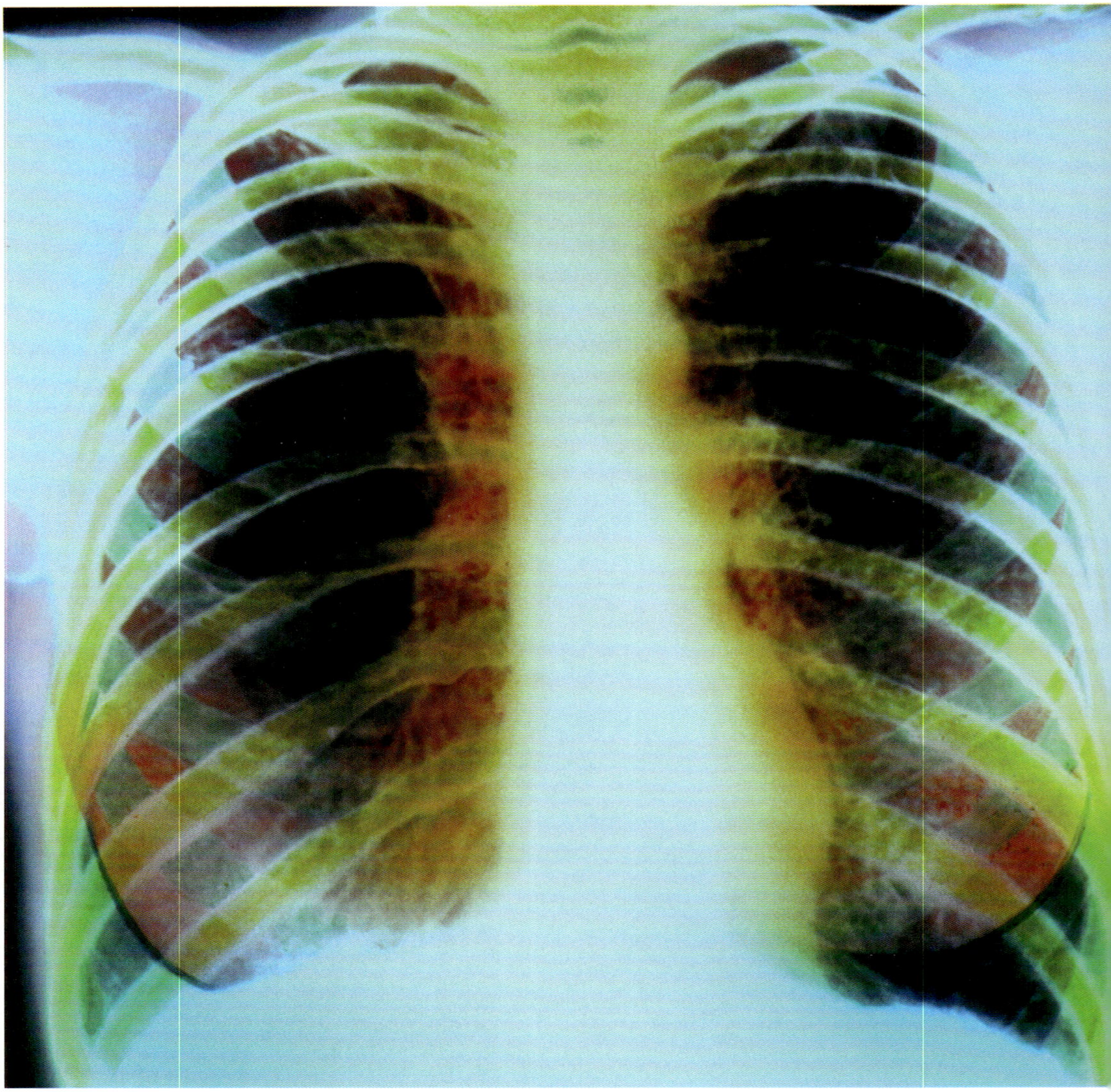

This chest X-ray shows the lungs of a person suffering from cystic fibrosis. Here, repeated infection has caused the bronchial walls within the lungs (*orange*) on either side of the spine (*center*) to thicken.

four thousand hereditary diseases, including sickle cell anemia, Tay-Sachs, and cystic fibrosis.

Cystic fibrosis is the most common inherited fatal disease in the United States, with one in thirty-one people being carriers. It is a recessive disease, caused by a mutated gene on chromosome 7. The cystic fibrosis gene leads to a defective protein that was supposed to regulate chloride and sodium in lung cells and other organ cells. With the protein broken, a salt imbalance causes the mucus in the lungs to thicken. It clogs the airways, making it difficult to breathe and leading to infections. In the 1950s, patients with cystic fibrosis typically died in early childhood. With new treatments, the life expectancy is 37.5. However, that depends on the severity of the disease in the patient. When a couple knows that one could be a carrier (because a sibling had cystic fibrosis), they may seek genetic counseling prior to having a baby. They face tough decisions on what to do with the information. One day the genome could provide a fix for these diseases.

With increasing knowledge of the genome, a cure for cystic fibrosis seems likely. Through gene therapy, doctors have loaded a working copy of the CF gene into a virus incapable of causing disease but still able to enter cells. This virus was used as a delivery system, or vector, for getting the working gene into the lung cells of cystic fibrosis patients. After injecting the virus into the lungs, they hoped it would enter the patient's lung cells and insert the working gene into the existing cells where it would be expressed. Gene therapy hasn't worked for cystic fibrosis so far. One problem is that lung viruses don't spread fast enough. Scientists are now trying to evolve viruses in the lab so that they will spread faster, which should make gene therapy more effective. They're also studying a gene that lessons the severity of the disease, which could lead to new treatments and a longer lifespan for these patients.

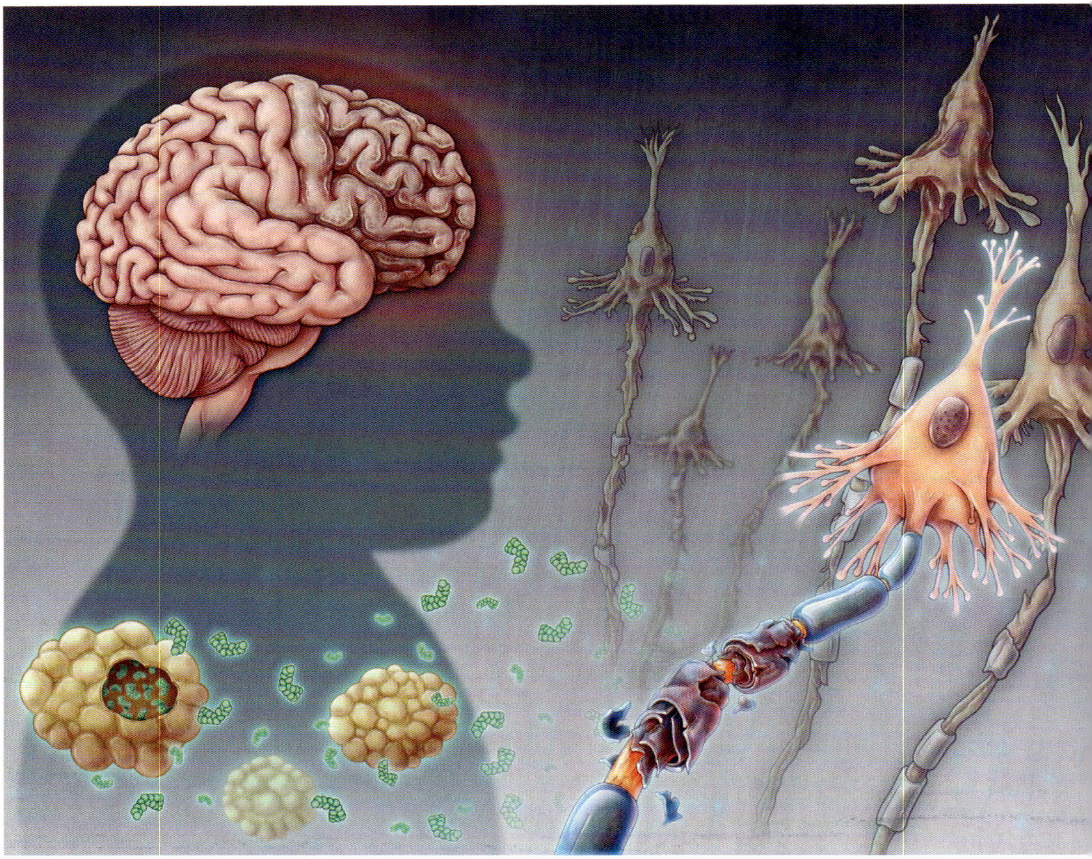

Tay-Sachs disease causes damage to nerve cells in the brain and spinal cord. This damage results in muscle weakness, vision and hearing loss, seizures, and paralysis.

Tay-Sachs is another genetic disease for which couples may get genetic testing. Tay-Sachs results from one letter in three billion being wrong. It is one of the most tragic diseases a child can have. A mutated gene affects the structure of the enzyme hexosaminidase A (HexA), which should break down a fatty substance in the brain. Instead, the substance accumulates in nerve cells. The nerves cannot transmit signals. Parents see the baby change. He loses his ability to laugh. Soon, he can't move. Even as he grows older, he needs to be cared for like a baby. At about six years old, the child dies.

Among the Ashkenazi Jewish population, one in twenty-seven people are carriers. A recessive disease, both parents need to be carriers for their child to get it. One man in the Orthodox Jewish community of Williamsburg in Brooklyn, Rabbi Joseph Ekstein,

GENES AND AGING

Genes can affect a person's health positively, too. If members of a family live to an old age, they may have genes that inhibit the production of free radicals, preventing cells from getting damaged by oxygen. They may also have long repeats at the beginning of each chromosome. When the genome is copied as cells divide throughout a person's life, these repeats tend to get left off. When they vanish, important letters eventually get erased. The longer a person's repeats, the less this process damages his or her genes. In this way, living a long life is thought to be at least partially hereditary.

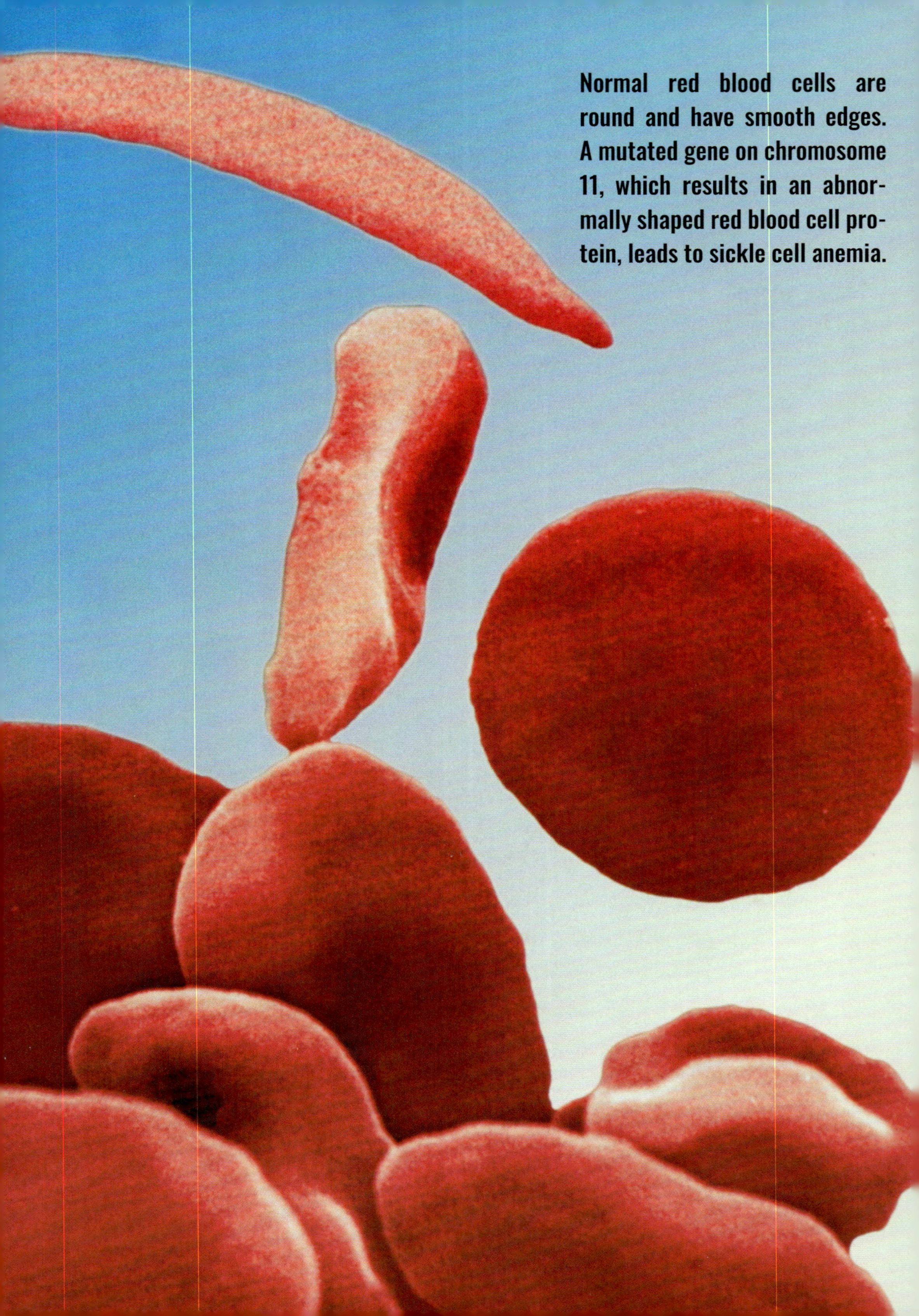

Normal red blood cells are round and have smooth edges. A mutated gene on chromosome 11, which results in an abnormally shaped red blood cell protein, leads to sickle cell anemia.

watched four of his eleven children suffer from the disease. He started a matchmaking program to prevent the disease from recurring in his community. Part of the matchmaking process involves blood testing for the Tay-Sachs gene. If both people in a potential couple have the gene, the matchmaker doesn't go forward with the match. Today no child is born with Tay-Sachs in the rabbi's neighborhood, and the program has expanded elsewhere.

Why Do Genetic Diseases Get Passed On?

There's no question that genetic diseases can have tragic results. But here's something to consider: historically, they might have had no effect. And, though we are taught to think that diseases are bad, some might have even helped people survive. Diabetes, for instance, is an epidemic in America, where food is plentiful. In the past, however, it may have helped people survive famine because they were better able to store starches and sugars.

Keep in mind that everybody has the genes linked to diseases. Only the altered genes cause a disease. Some mutations can cause one disease and prevent another. Often, the disease that is prevented was once an epidemic. Being a carrier for Tay-Sachs, for example, can make a person more resistant to tuberculosis (TB), a dangerous epidemic in the past for people, including Ashkenazi Jews, living in crowded cities. Today TB is treatable.

Sickle cell anemia is a disease in which red blood cells are sickle shaped, clogging blood vessels and causing infections, organ damage, and chronic pain and fatigue. In the United States, the disease is most common among African Americans. Being a carrier for sickle cell anemia, however, seems to provide some resistance to malaria, a disease that has plagued sub-Saharan Africa. Malaria has been eliminated in the United States, and could be eradicated worldwide with the preventative medicine available today.

In the United States, these resistances are not helpful today, so there is no "good side" to the diseases. However, it explains why natural selection allowed the mutations to spread through generations.

7

Using Genomic Information

Now that the human genome has been sequenced, people need to decide how this information can and should be used. Doctors and scientists can use an individual's DNA sequence to diagnose and treat disease. But should employers and insurance companies have access to the information in a person's genetic makeup?

Public Policy and the Genome

Leaders of the National Human Genome Research Institute knew that ethical issues would arise from the Human Genome Project. In 1990 they established ELSI, the Ethical, Legal, and Social Implications research program. It addresses topics such as intellectual property, genetic research methods, and genetics in healthcare. In May of 2008, ELSI achieved an important goal when the Genetic Information Nondiscrimination Act became law. This protects patients against employment or insurance discrimination based on their genetic information. The group continues to work for the protection of patient privacy, guidelines for expanding genomic testing, and other ethical practices surrounding the use of genetic information.

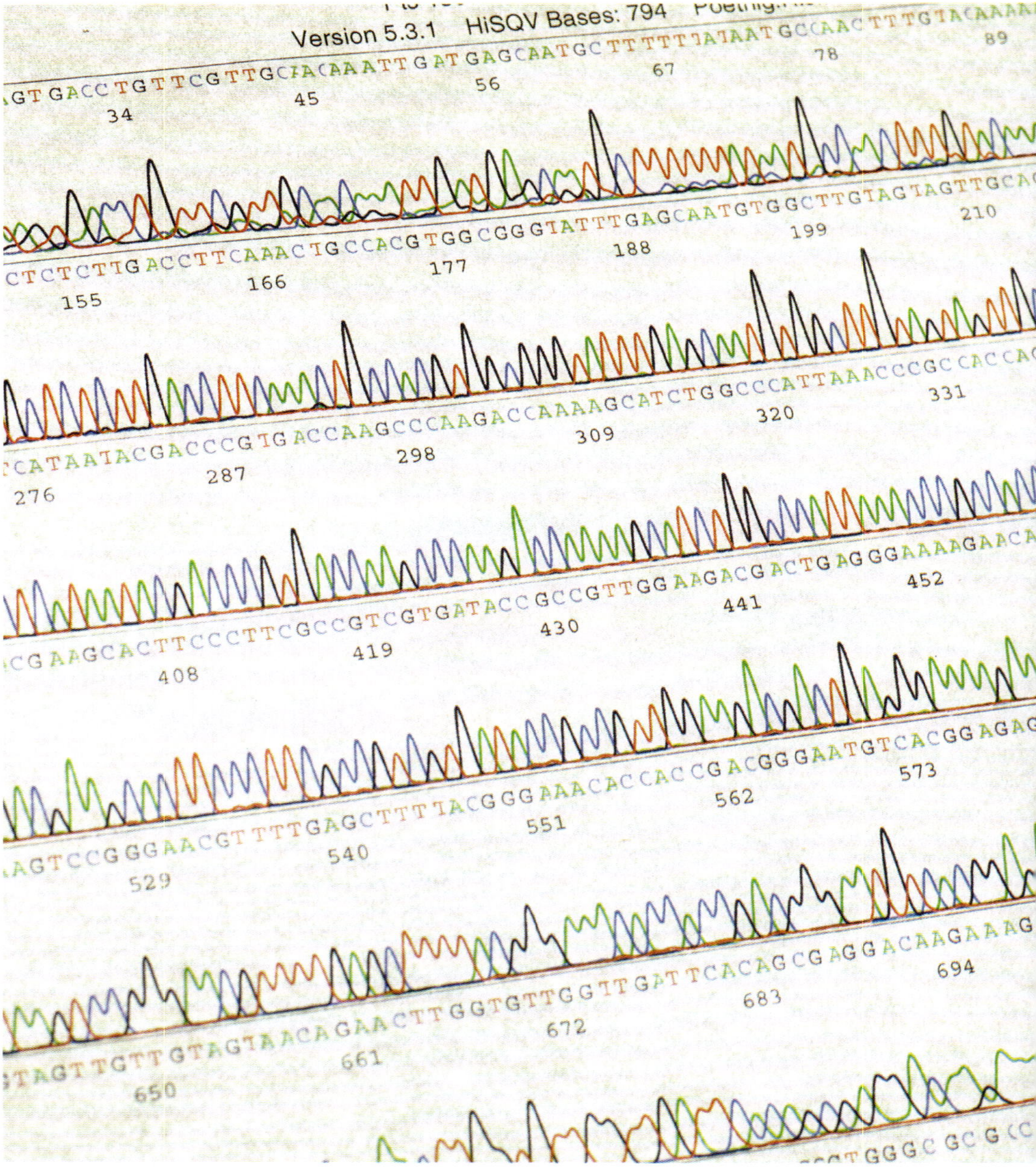

A DNA sequence reveals the order of all the base pairs in an individual's genome, revealing the unique blueprint used to create that individual.

One ethical debate was whether or not the discovery of a particular gene or gene sequence could be considered intellectual property. Many companies are developing diagnostic tests and treatments based on genetic knowledge. Should they be able to patent a gene found in the human body?

At first glance, people probably would think not. They didn't invent human genes. Scientists could not simply look at a gene and declare it theirs. In order for it to be patented, it had to be isolated and purified, and the scientists had to have a purpose for the patent—that the gene will be used to develop a diagnostic test, for instance. Companies argued that patents would make innovation financially possible. Research and development of gene-related tests and treatments cost money. Research companies and universities want to earn back the money they invested. Fearing that competitors will make the same product discourages research and development.

By the same token, too many patents could discourage research and development. Scientists wanting to research a genetic disease may find the licensing fees too expensive. Or scientists may worry that they will research a gene, only to learn halfway through that the gene has just been patented. The United States Supreme Court settled this argument in 2013 by declaring human genes a "product of nature." The Court determined that nothing new was created when a gene was discovered. Therefore, there was no intellectual property to protect. As a result, human genes can no longer be patented.

Individual Decisions

Some genetic decisions involve more personal choices. Genetic tests for more than one thousand diseases are available to patients. Deciding whether to be tested (or have a child tested) forces

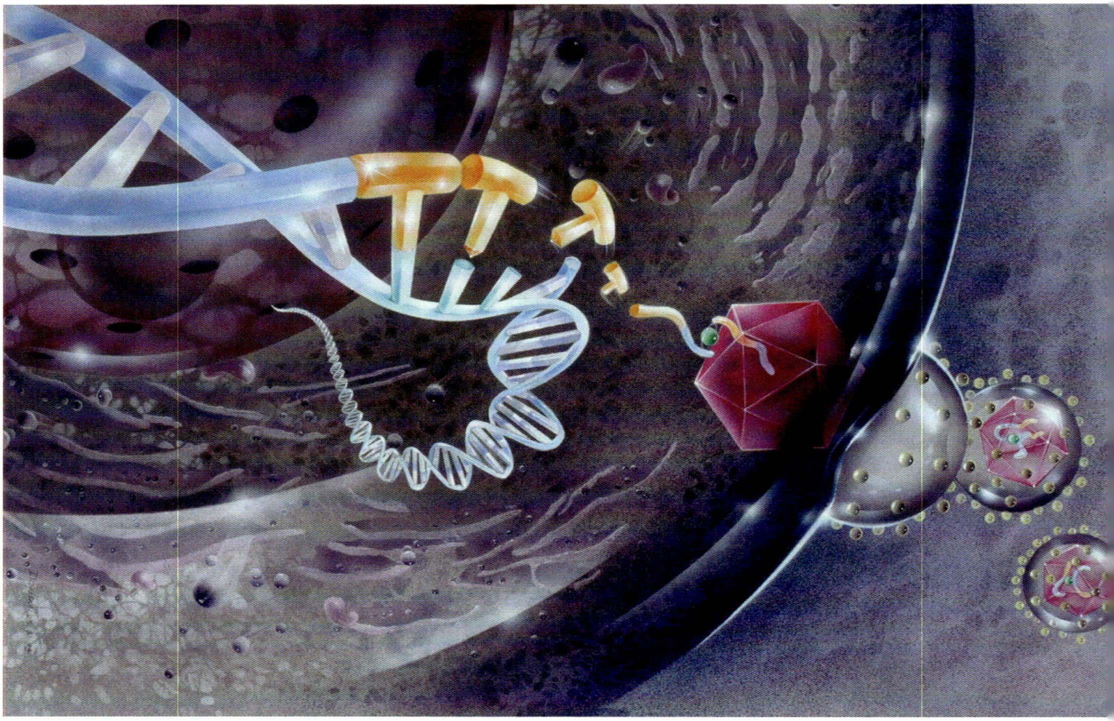

Gene therapy is one of the gene-related treatments under investigation. In this process, a virus delivers a normal copy of a gene along with the molecular machinery needed to replace the damaged one.

people to make tough decisions. For instance, should tests be provided for diseases that have no cure? What should a person do with the information, and how might it alter his or her life? This is particularly an issue in the case of disease for which multiple genes play a role. If patients are told they have a gene associated with a particular deadly disease but that this is no guarantee they will actually get the disease, will the information negatively impact their lives unnecessarily?

Huntington's tests have been available for a long time. In the case of dominant diseases like Huntingon's, if the test is positive,

PERSONALIZED MEDICINE

Once upon a time, doctors treated everyone with the same medical condition with the same drugs. If that treatment didn't work, they tried another one. The Human Genome Project is beginning to change these days of trial-and-error treatment.

Since the completion of the Human Genome Project, researchers have discovered more than eighteen hundred disease genes. They have also discovered that an individual's genetic makeup affects how he or she responds to different medications.

Personalized medicine, or genomic medicine, is a treatment plan based on the information found in an individual's DNA sequence. This approach is not only for the sick. It can also be used to give people information about their disease risks, allowing them to make changes in their lifestyles before they get sick.

nothing can be done about it. Some people don't want to know. A positive result would be too devastating. Others do. Adults are free to request information about their own health. But what if a twelve-year-old wants to know if he or she has the CAG repeat that causes Huntington's? Or if his or her parents want to know? The American Society of Human Genetics (ASHG) recommends genetic testing of minors only if a diagnosis is in the best interest of the child. In other words, testing should only be done if it would help treat the disease. Because there is no treatment for Huntington's disease, the ASHG recommends deferring testing until the child reaches adulthood. But, ultimately, the decision of whether or not to be tested is up to the patient and his or her parents.

Looking on the flip side, is it unethical not to test for some diseases? Rabbi Ekstein argued that it was unethical *not* to be tested for the Tay-Sachs gene prior to marriage. Why refuse a test that would save a baby from a harmful disease, he argued.

Testing for the health of a baby is a sensitive issue for people who may be carriers. Some people want to be tested before they conceive. However, if both the husband and wife are carriers, they might still want to have children. Options include pre-implantation genetic diagnosis (PGD). In this case, embryos are created in vitro using the mother's egg and the father's sperm. The DNA of the early embryos is then tested for the genetic mutation they are at risk for, such as one that causes cystic fibrosis or Huntington's disease. Only the mutation-free embryos are implanted.

Today all pregnant women are routinely offered screening for Down syndrome. But it is the woman's choice whether to be tested and, if the results are positive, whether to proceed with the pregnancy.

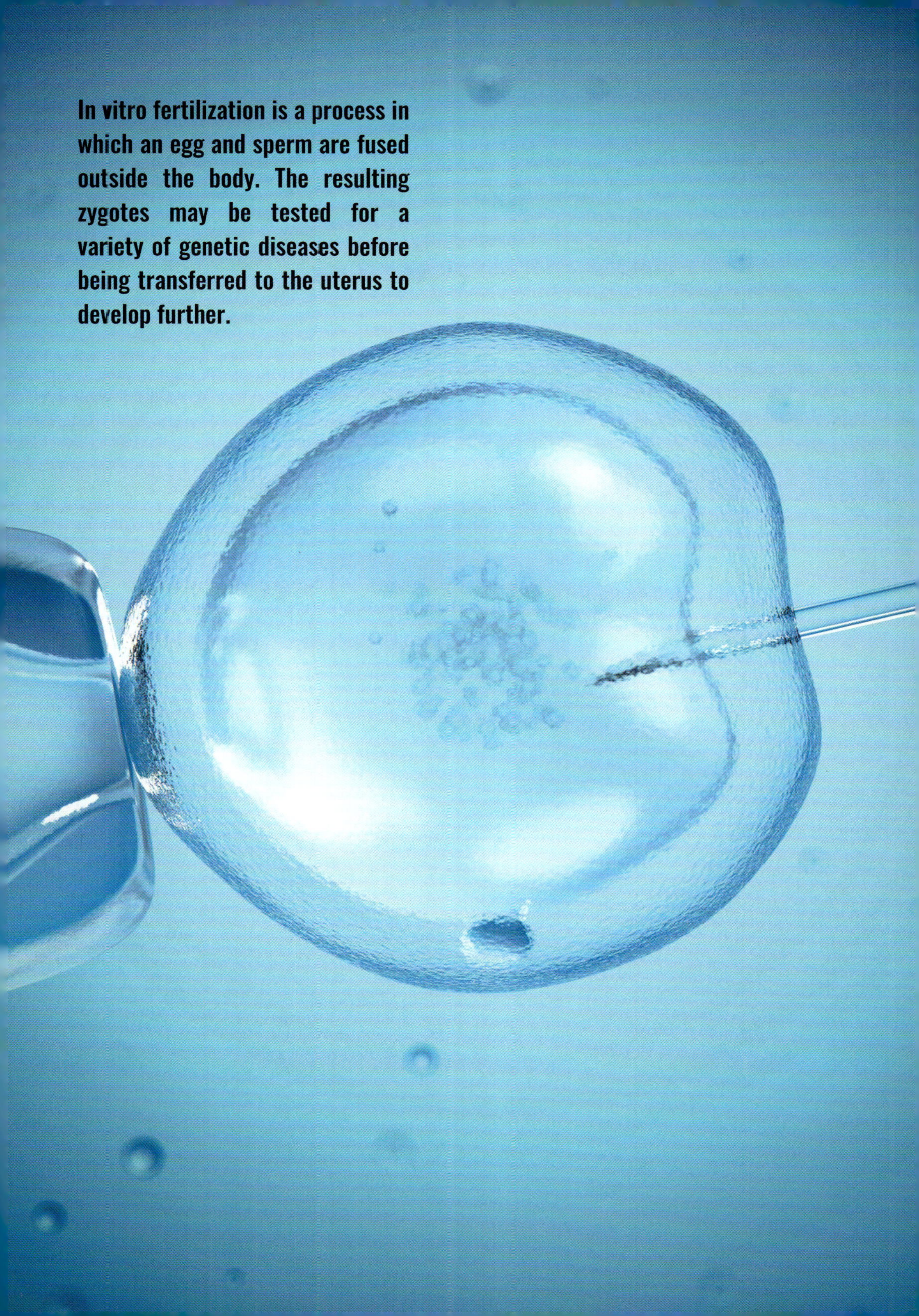

In vitro fertilization is a process in which an egg and sperm are fused outside the body. The resulting zygotes may be tested for a variety of genetic diseases before being transferred to the uterus to develop further.

People have strong feelings about the ethics of testing fetuses. Their opinions might depend on their view of disabilities. If they think people with Down syndrome have a good quality of life, as many of them do, they might think a trisomy-21 screening test is unnecessary. If somebody in their family suffers from painful disease, they might think genetic counseling or PGD is a good idea for couples at risk.

In the end, it is up to the individual to make these difficult decisions. Doctors hope that, in the future, parents will be offered not only genetic tests for their children, but genetic cures, as well.

8

What's Next?

Now that the human genome has been sequenced, scientists have a list of DNA base pairs. (In fact, everybody does. It's available for public viewing on the internet.) But they don't yet know the function of every gene. They don't know how all the genes work together to build proteins. And they don't fully understand how proteins work together to build humans. Mapping the genome was one of the biggest scientific accomplishments of all time. But it was only the first step.

Next Steps

Genomic scientists are now working to understand the genome and how it works in greater depth. One of the things they are studying is how genomes vary among people. Haplogroups represent people who share similar variations in their genomes. These variations might explain why different groups get different diseases.

Understanding haplogroups and how they differ has also helped scientists understand how *Homo sapiens* have evolved. Using the gene variations between groups of people, scientists have mapped the migration patterns of ancient humans. As more

World Map of Y-DNA Haplogroups
Dominant Haplogroups in Native Populations
with Possible Migration Routes

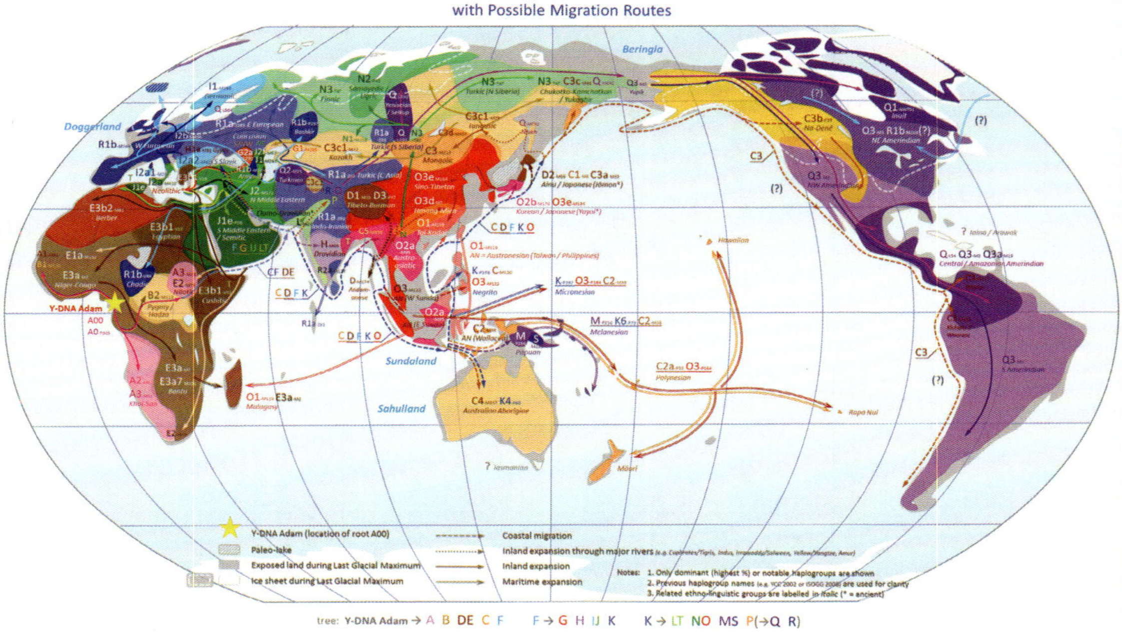

By studying variations in genomes, scientists can retrace ancient human migration patterns.

people get their genomes sequenced, this understanding will continue to grow.

Proteomics, or the location, interaction, structure, and function of proteins, is also an ongoing area of study. Determining the structures of all human proteins will be a bigger job than sequencing the genome. The genome sequence is linear. It can be read like a book. Proteins are three-dimensional. Studying proteins is important, however, as diseases may be curable through protein therapy.

Researchers are also looking into how the physical structure of our genome affects its function. The DNA double helix is wrapped around protein molecules to form a nucleosome, which makes a thread called chromatin. When cells are copied, chromatin loops and coils to make chromosomes. Scientists have found that the shape of the genome shifts over time. The changing shape allows various segments of DNA to interact at different times. In part, scientists think these interactions determine the timing of cell functions.

Scientists are also working on understating how genes are related to each other. For example, they have learned that diseases caused by a single base pair mutation, such as cystic fibrosis,

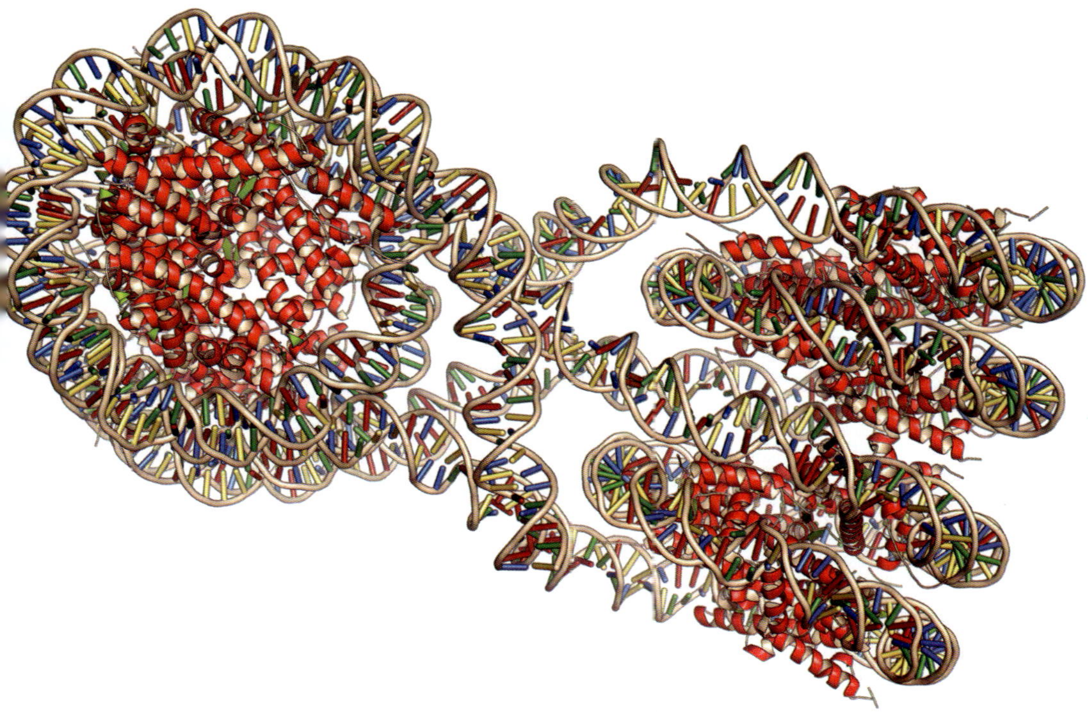

If all the DNA in a human genome is stretched out, it would reach to the sun and back more than three hundred times. To make all this fit into a tiny cell, the DNA is wrapped around proteins and then coiled into a structure called a nucleosome.

can be modified by other genes. These influences have been found to change the phenotype of people with these diseases. Understanding how this occurs may lead to better treatments.

As technology improves, DNA sequencing is getting faster. It took years for the first human genome to be mapped. Now, genome sequencing can routinely be done in a little more than a day. New instruments are reducing that time to as little as an hour. As the process gets faster, it becomes cheaper and available to more people.

In the future, a doctor could have patients' genomes on file and advise them about what lifestyle choices may improve their health. For instance, for some people, such as those with genes that make them susceptible to heart disease, a doctor could prescribe a low-cholesterol, low fat diet. Other people may not need this type of diet, assuming they stay at a healthy weight.

Individualized Medicine

Knowledge of the genome is already revolutionizing cancer treatment. Cancer grows if a gene called an oncogene is jammed on, and a tumor suppressor gene is jammed off. These conditions can allow a cell to grow and divide uncontrollably. At that point, the TP53 gene on chromosome 17, which encodes protein P53, tells cancerous cells to commit suicide, a process known as apoptosis. People with one faulty TP53 gene have a higher chance of getting cancer as these uncontrollably dividing cells are not signaled appropriately to self-destruct.

Scientists used to think radiation and chemotherapy treated cancer because it killed cancer cells by damaging their DNA. In fact, the damage isn't enough to kill the cells. It's only enough to alert P53, which tells the multiplying cells to dismantle themselves. If TP53 is damaged, chemotherapy doesn't work because P53

This is a colored scanning electron micrograph (SEM) of a pancreatic cancer cell. Cancer is caused when cells begin to divide at an abnormal rate and are not destroyed by proteins that usually carry out that function.

can't order the cells to commit suicide. Scientist have developed and are testing treatments to restore the faulty TP53 gene so the body can once again order cancerous cells to dismantle.

Gene therapy offers hope for curing other diseases, too. It has already been used effectively to treat children with severe combined immune deficiency (SCID). This condition once required children to live their lives in a germ-free bubble because SCID causes them to be exceptionally prone to infections they cannot fight off. Now, with gene therapy and other interventions, they can lead more normal lives. Scientists believe gene therapy will also work for diseases such as Lou Gehrig's, Alzheimer's, and cystic fibrosis. It is a matter of discovering the right method for each disease.

EDITING THE GENOME

Using a system known as CRISPR, scientists can now edit the human genome, too. CRISPR works by searching for a specific DNA sequence and snipping it out. This allows researchers to correct mutations or delete genes that cause disease. They can also add genes that lessen the effects of a disease. In November 2017, scientists attempted genome editing inside a patient's body for the first time. This technology is still being tested to see if it works and if it is safe. If it works, scientists hope to use it to treat, and possibly cure, hemophilia, sickle cell disease, and other inherited conditions in the future.

Scientists continue their search for a better understanding of the genome, the proteome, and how these two systems work together to create a human being. As the medical industry builds on the knowledge gained, advances in individualized disease prevention and treatment is expected to grow. An increasing number of at-home genetic testing kits are already available for people who are interested in obtaining a better understanding their health risks and their ancestry. However, scientists and doctors both urge caution when using these services. The social implications of direct-to-consumer DNA testing have not yet been fully explored. People who use at-home testing kits need to thoroughly understand how testing companies are using their results and the privacy risks that may accompany DNA testing.

Bibliography

American Association for the Advancement of Science. "The Cells in Your Body." Science NetLinks. Retrieved November 14, 2017. http://sciencenetlinks.com/student-teacher-sheets/cells-your-body.

Callaway, Ewen. "Genetic Adam and Eve Did Not Live Too Far Apart in Time." *Nature*, August 6, 2013. Retrieved November 28, 2017. https://www.nature.com/news/genetic-adam-and-eve-did-not-live-too-far-apart-in-time-1.13478.

Chi, Kelly Rae. "The Dark Side of the Human Genome." *Nature*, October 24, 2016. Retrieved November 14, 2017. https://www.nature.com/articles/538275a.

Dennis, Carina, and Richard Gallagher, ed. *The Human Genome*. New York, NY: Nature Publishing Group, 2001.

Gibbons, Ann. "Humans Mated with Neandertals Much Earlier and More Frequently than Thought." *Science*, February 17, 2016. Retrieved November 30, 2017. http://www.sciencemag.org/news/2016/02/humans-mated-neandertals-much-earlier-and-more-frequently-thought.

Hamers, Laurel. "Scientists Find Clue to Why Mitochondrial DNA Comes Only from Mom." *Science News,* June 23, 2016. Retrieved November 27, 2017. https://www.sciencenews.org/article/scientists-find-clue-why-mitochondrial-dna-comes-only-mom.

Harris, Richard. "Which Genes Make You Taller? A Whole Bunch of Them, It Turns Out." *All Things Considered*, National Public Radio, February 1, 2017. Retrieved November 28, 2017. https://www.npr.org/sections/health-shots/2017/02/01/512859830/which-genes-make-you-taller-a-whole-lot-it-turns-out.

Hewings-Martin, Yella. "How Many Cells Are in the Human Body?" *MedicalNewsToday*, July 12, 2017. Retrieved November 14, 2017. https://www.medicalnewstoday.com/articles/318342.php.

Kimball, John W. "Transposons: Mobile DNA." Kimball's Biology Pages, August 2, 2017. Retrieved November 14, 2017. http://www.biology-pages.info/T/Transposons.html.

Mayell, Hillary. "Three High-Altitude Peoples, Three Adaptations to Thin Air." National Geographic News, February 25, 2004. Retrieved November 27, 2017. https://news.nationalgeographic.com/news/2004/02/0224_040225_evolution.html.

McElheny, Victor K. *Drawing the Map of Life: Inside the Human Genome Project*. Philadelphia, PA: Basic Books, 2010.

Mukherjee, Siddhartha. *The Gene: An Intimate History*. New York, NY: Scribner, 2016.

National Down Syndrome Society. "Fact Sheet." Retrieved November 28, 2017. http://www.ndss.org/index.php?option=com_content&view=category&id=35&Itemid=57.

National Human Genome Research Institute. ELSI Research Program. Retrieved November 28, 2017. http://www.genome.gov/10001618.

Phenomena. "The Smell of Evolution." National Geographic, December 11, 2013. Retrieved November 16, 2017. http://

phenomena.nationalgeographic.com/2013/12/11/the-smell-of-evolution.

Ponomarenko, Elena A. et al. “The Size of the Human Proteome: The Width and Depth.” *International Journal of Analytical Chemistry*, May 19, 2016. Retrieved November 14, 2017. https://www.ncbi.nlm.nih.gov/pmc/articles/PMC4889822.

Ramsey, Lydia, and Samantha Lee. “Our DNA Is 99.9% the Same as the Person Sitting Next to Us—and We’re Surprisingly Similar to a Bunch of Other Living Things.” *Business Insider*, May 6, 2016. Retrieved November 14, 2017. http://www.businessinsider.com/comparing-genetic-similarity-between-humans-and-other-things-2016-5.

Rettner, Rachael. “Epigenetics: Definition & Examples.” *Live Science*, June 24, 2013. Retrieved November 27, 2017. https://www.livescience.com/37703-epigenetics.html.

Reynolds, Gretchen. “The Genetics of Being a Daredevil.” *New York Times*, February 19, 2014. Retrieved November 28, 2017. https://well.blogs.nytimes.com/2014/02/19/the-genetics-of-being-a-daredevil.

Shampo, Marc, and Robert Kyle. “J. Craig Venter—The Human Genome Project.” *May Clinic Proceedings*, April 2011. Retrieved November 30, 2017. https://www.ncbi.nlm.nih.gov/pmc/articles/PMC3068906/.

Technologist Online. “First Maps of the Human Proteome to Unlock ‘Mystery of Life.’” March 5, 2015. Retrieved November 14, 2017. http://www.technologist.eu/first-maps-of-the-human-proteome-to-unlock-mystery-of-life.

Glossary

apoptosis Programmed cell death that occurs as a natural part of growth and development.

cell A small unit of protoplasm that usually has a nucleus containing an individual's entire genome, cytoplasm, and a membrane.

chromosomes The microscopic rods that form during cell division and contain DNA.

DNA (deoxyribonucleic acid) The chemical compound that contains instructions for building proteins.

dominant gene A gene that affects phenotype if one copy is inherited.

exon A nucleotide sequence within a gene that codes for amino acids to build a protein.

gamete A sex cell; in animals, either a sperm or egg.

gene A string of nucleotide bases that gives instructions for making a protein.

gene therapy A disease treatment in which doctors insert a working copy of a gene into a harmless virus and infect the patient, in hopes that the healthy gene cells will insert their code into the existing cells.

genetic drift The process by which genetic changes spread through a population due to chance.

genotype A person's entire collection of genes, expressed or not.

germ cell A cell that becomes a gamete.

Homo sapiens The only living species of humans.

Human Genome Project A government-funded program through which scientists mapped the human genome.

intron A nucleotide sequence within a gene that does not code for amino acids.

meiosis A type of cell division that results in gametes with half the number of chromosomes that a somatic cell has.

mutation A change in DNA sequence, which may be helpful, harmful, or have no effect.

natural selection The process by which animals develop genetic mutations that result in higher birthrates, causing the mutation to spread throughout the population.

nucleotide bases The four chemicals that make up the DNA code: adenine, cytosine, guanine, thymine. In threes, they make up a code for amino acids.

oncogene A gene that, when stuck "on," can allow a cell to grow and divide out of control.

phenotype The physical results of the genes that are expressed in an individual.

protein A chemical substance made up of amino acids. They provide the structure and facilitate the processes of living things.

proteome The entire set of proteins coded for in the genome.

recessive gene A gene requiring two copies, one from each parent, in order for it to affect phenotype.

ribosome A molecular machine that makes proteins out of amino acids.

RNA (ribonucleic acid) A long chain of nucleotides found in cells. Messenger RNA carries copies of DNA to the cell cytoplasm to be translated into amino acids.

somatic cell Any cell that does not become a gamete.

transcription The process of creating an equivalent RNA copy of a sequence of DNA.

translation The first stage of protein biosynthesis, during which proteins are produced by decoding the mRNA produced in transcription.

transposons Sequences of DNA that can move around to different positions within the genome of a single cell, a process called transposition.

vector A virus or other organism that acts as a vehicle to deliver genetic material into another cell.

zygote A fertilized egg.

Further Reading

Books

Bond, David. *Genetic Engineering*. Broomall, PA: Mason Crest, 2017.

Gerdes, Louise I. *Human Genetics*. Farmington Hills, MI: Greenhaven Press, 2014.

Gibson, Karen Bush. *Cells: Experience Life at Its Tiniest*. White River Junction, VT: Nomad Press, 2017.

Harris, Eugene E. *Ancestors in Our Genome: The New Science of Human Evolution*. New York, NY: Oxford University Press, 2014.

Jackson, Tom. *Genetics: Why We Are Who We Are*. New York, NY: Cavendish Square, 2017.

Lew, Kristi. *Genetic Ancestry Testing*. New York, NY: Enslow Publishing, 2018.

Mooney, Carla. *Genetics: Breaking the Code of Your DNA*. White River Junction, VT: Nomad Press, 2014.

Websites

Genetics Home Reference

ghr.nlm.nih.gov

This part of the National Institute of Health's Library of Medicine provides information about how genetics affects human health.

National Human Genome Research Institute

www.genome.gov

The National Human Genome Research Institute is the division of the National Institute of Health that conducts and supports genomic research.

Understanding Evolution

evolution.berkeley.edu/evolibrary/home.php

This educational website is run by the University of California Museum of Paleontology to help people understand how evolution works and how changes in the genome can drive it.

Index

A

C

D

E

F

G

H

I

L

M

N

O

P

R

S

T

V

W

Z